The Money Man - Volume 1

M.J. O'Doul

For Josie

CHAPTER 1

The jagged crevice in the static hours where recollections go to die. That perfect locus of the night before's misadventure and the morning after's regret, crossing but never really touching. Anywhere else the quiet stillness of this moment would shake the melancholy from the nascent morning air. But here every hour looks the same for all semblance of time is lost in a in a dizzying neon-dazzle haze.

Las Vegas.

Treasure Island casino bar. I sit alone, beer in hand, watching the world or something like it go by while multicoloured bottles of exotic booze illuminate the periphery. It's six in the morning, yet the town is blissfully unaware as it makes and breaks patrons with a feral, rabid intensity as though it's still the drip of the night's buzz. All around me lights flash, wheels spin, chips crash and wallets thin.

And there she was.

Lola.

But where was I?

Cool, calm and content I'm perched, the most I've been in many months, as the waves of glory from a wild night that ended just over an hour ago wash over me.

My friends have all gone upstairs to bed, but I still have oil to burn. The last remnants from months of frustration with a life more ordinary back in London. Angst which quickly began to dissipate in San Francisco, ailed in LA and all but died under the glare of the strip club's blue lights in the small hours of this morning.

As I take a tentative swig of the slowly warming ale from the cool bottle, a charming voice materialises over my right shoulder.

'Hi.'

Gleefully startled, I turn across out of curiosity to greet her.

And she is a vision.

A petite yet voluptuous figure in tight blue jeans, somewhat reminiscent of a young Jennifer Lopez, and a sleeveless beige top which fits her form beautifully. With her big brown eyes, generous pouting lips and soft cappuccino-coloured skin, she is a Venus unlike any I have ever seen. Bearing a sultry mixture of Spanish, Taino and negligible African features, she is every bit as striking as they come. After one casual flick of her lustrous ponytail, my guard drops, and I am entranced.

'Hello you.'

'How you doing?'

'I'm great, thanks. I've been out all night with the boys, so I'm just chilling now. Keeping the party going on my own, I guess.'

'I like your accent. Where are you from?'

'London. London, England. I'm out here with some friends on a road trip, celebrating my best friend's 30th. We started out in San Francisco last week, then from San Fran' to Monterey, San Simeon, LA. Now here we are.'

'Wow, nice. That sounds like fun. How do you like it here?'

'I absolutely love it. This is my first time in America, and I want to stay. I don't want to go back home on Sunday. I'm Michael by the way.'

'Lola.'

'Nice to meet you Lola, and might I say you look rather lovely today.' I gently extend my right hand, prompting Lola to do the same. After placing her hand in mine, I plant a tiny kiss upon it, prompting Lola to giggle and blush.

'Oh, thank you. You're such a gentleman!' gushes Lola.

'So, Lola, tell me about yourself. Starting with that tattoo there. It's very nice. What does it say?'

'Oh' says Lola in response, surprised and looking down at the stylised cursive black ink on her right arm. 'Sexy Lexi. It's an old nickname my friends gave me back in the day in Pittsburgh.'

'You're from Pittsburgh? Pittsburgh, Pennsylvania? Lovely.'

'Yeah, but I've been living out here for a few weeks now. My apartment's just 25 minutes away from the strip. So, Vegas is home now. Both of my parents are Puerto Rican, 100%.'

'Puerto Rican, like Jennifer Lopez?'

'Oh yeah, I'm representing like J-Lo!'

'Nice. I like it.'

'I was looking at your cowboy hat. It's really nice. Where did you get it?'

'I got this from the Grand Canyon' I reply while playfully tipping my hat towards Lola. 'We did the tour yesterday, Hoover Dam and Grand Canyon. It was amazing. When we got to the Grand Canyon, we did the Skywalk and one of my friends and I stood on the highest peak, 4,000 feet in the air. We were up there on this rock, there's barely enough room for the both of us. A little mouse starts running around beneath our feet and I'm standing there wearing these blue suede shoes that you see on me now, which have absolutely no support. I was so scared, but I felt so alive.'

'Wow, that's incredible!' blurts Lola, laughing. 'I can't imagine being all the way up there, especially in those Elvis shoes of yours, ha ha ha! You know what, I would love to go to the Grand Canyon! It sounds so me!'

'You would absolutely love it, Lola. It's absolutely brilliant. While we were there, we took a wagon ride with these cowboys, and we got to handle guns. Real guns. They weren't loaded but it was so cool. I was throwing them from one hand to the other, spinning them, pretending I was Neo with the two guns in slow-motion. Before that I'd never held a gun in my life. Never. It was amazing.'

'You're becoming quite the cowboy. The guns, the hat. Where have you parked up the horse?'

We laugh heartily in unison before I raise my beer bottle with my right hand in a toasting gesture. 'To the horse!'

'Ha ha, yes. To the horse!'

I take a quick sip of O'Doul's before quietly examining the bottle's depleting content and placing it back on the bar.

'Tell me, what brings you to Vegas? What do you do?'

'I'm a dancer. I did that for quite a few years back home and now I'm trying to do that out here. Wanna get myself out there, do my thing, make some money. Enough to invest for the future.'

'What kind of dancing?'

'I'm a stripper.'

Immediately I'm happily taken aback by Lola's answer, as well as her nonchalant delivery. 'Oh, wow. You know what? It's funny you should say that because we were out all night at Sapphires. Didn't leave there until five. We had a great time. I reckon you'd do really well there. Have you been?'

'No, I can't say that I have yet. I'll have to check it out though. Sounds like fun.'

'It was so much fun. I took my friend whose birthday it is to the VIP lounge, and we got some dances in there.'

'That's quite a birthday present.'

'Well, you're only 30 once, just as I'll be in February.'

'You're twenty-nine? Wow, you look so much younger!'

'Ah, you're too kind. How old are you, Lola?'

'24. I'm a baby.'

'You're in your prime. Not like me, ha ha. So, tell me, where are you dancing at the moment?'

'I'm not dancing anywhere right now. It's hard in Vegas because you need a license to dance here.'

'A license? No way.'

'Yeah. Out here it's so different from back home because there's so much more money to be made.'

'I can imagine. Still, it beats being an accountant.'

'But you accountants will always make money. Not like us. We're a luxury, so to speak.'

'You've got me there. When times are good, people need us to look after all their money. When times are bad, people need us to look after what little they have left so they can spend it to make more.'

'Sounds like you've got it all worked out. I like a man with a plan.'

'It's alright. It has its moments.'

'So, Michael, what's your background?'

'My mum is from Ireland and my dad is from Barbados, but I've lived in England all my life.'

'Ah. That's a nice mixture.'

'Yeah. I also have a Greek Godfather and a Jewish Godmother.'

'Hmmm. Interesting. Anyway, I was thinking....'

'Yes?'

'If you want, I could dance for you up in your room. Do you have a big room upstairs?'

'I do. Yes. I have a lovely room up on the 25th floor.'

'Sounds great. Shall we go?'

'Yes, let's. I'd love to. Oh, I've just remembered something. My roommate is asleep up there. That means we're going to have to use the bathroom. Hope that's OK. It's a very spacious bathroom, I can assure you.'

'Yeah, sure. That's not a problem' replies Lola with a nod and a wry smile. I quickly gulp down the last of my beer before pushing the empty bottle to the left with my right hand.

'Just one more thing before we go upstairs, Lola. Are you camera-shy?' A look of surprise and mild horror escapes briefly from Lola's luminous smile, prompting me to break the slightly awkward silence with a gentle laugh. 'I meant for a photo, ha ha' I say while reaching into the inner left-hand pocket of my navy-blue suit jacket with my right-hand for my phone. 'No no no, I didn't mean anything like that, ha ha.' With the momentary tension now dissolved, the laughter quickly becomes mutual. I snap a series of photos in quick succession with my right thumb, starting before Lola has a chance to respond verbally, while my curvy companion playfully pouts for the camera.

'Lovely jubbly' I say whilst snapping the last few photos before springing out of my barstool. 'OK baby. Let's go.' I put my phone back into my pocket while Lola leaves her own barstool. Before walking up beside her, I take a moment to admire Lola's full, wide bottom, a prominent sight in denim with its roundness further accentuated by a small waist and wide, sloping hips above and thick, shapely thighs below. She is a picture of preternatural pulchritude, straight from the silver screen. I'm guessing 34-26-43.

I slide my left arm around Lola's waist, and we casually glide past the burly security guard towards the gleam of the golden elevator doors, laughing all the way. We briefly detach so I can push the button for the lift and quietly wait for it after the light comes on.

The lift doors open, and we bundle into the mirrored car before breaking into an overt display of lustful groping, giggling as we go along. I reach across Lola's lithe torso to press the button for the 25th floor with my right hand. The doors close and we're surrounded by other guests. Lola plays with my straw cowboy hat while I roughly grab her behind with my right palm, prompting a look of disapproval from a middle-aged woman over Lola's shoulder.

On the way up the bell sounds a few times. I'm oblivious to the faces of the people boarding and departing the lift, as well as the floors we stop on. All I know is that we're not on 25. My mind is on nothing but Lola and what we're going to do. Finally, the ping for 25 comes and we stride away from the crowd towards the floor.

'This way' I tell Lola while pointing with my right hand and leading her down a hallway that slopes diagonally to the right. I begin to walk half a step behind Lola as we pass several rooms on both sides. Along the way I enthusiastically smack and grab Lola's protruding posterior over and over again.

'I like your booty' I tell Lola, as cool as you like. 'Aw, thank you baby!' she replies with a giddy giggle. As we continue on our merry way, I can't keep my hands off her. After a few more moments we pull in on the left outside a door. We stand facing one another while I reach for my card key.

'Before we go inside, I need to know if you're carrying any alcohol or firearms' I say to Lola with a mock stern face betraying my jovial intentions just slightly. 'I'm not much of a drinker. I smoke weed occasionally, but that's about it.' As she says this, Lola rifles through her handbag to show me she is carrying no contraband.

'I'm kidding. That's just something one of the tour guides at the Grand Canyon said yesterday and it stuck with me.' We share a sweet laugh as I pull out the card key. For a brief moment we look into one another's eyes, my gaze filling up with silent anticipation as the last few nerves disperse like errant tumbleweed. I turn inwards and blast their debris with one swiftly eager swipe of the key card into the golden door handle.

The light turns green. It's showtime.

CHAPTER 2

And there she was.

Lola.

But where was I?

Who was I?

Michael O'Sullivan. 29 years old. Single. Management Accountant. Lives alone in a one-bedroom flat in Dagenham. Enjoys football, films, cooking, baking, reading, chess and most, of all, writing and performing poetry. Non-drinker, non-smoker (apart from the odd Cuban cigar). Known to also enjoy karaoke, especially when on my overseas travels. Proficient in Spanish & Italian with a rudimentary grasp of French.

If that comes across as a rather sterile online dating profile, well, there's a reason for that. I've regurgitated those same points in many a largely unread profile, along with the same photograph of myself in my tuxedo. Evoking James Bond vibes, eliciting Frank Spencer results. I can't tell you how many times my verbose introductory messages have been marked as read but never replied to. At this point in time, I have to work my way up to being unlucky in love.

Nothing really to report as far as the ladies are concerned, apart from sporadic encounters with escorts and strippers. Those started with a 22nd birthday trip to Brighton, my first time, and continued right through to this year's birthday trip to Amsterdam nine months ago. No childhood sweetheart. No little girlfriend. I have always been single. Christmas after Christmas went by with me vowing that next year would be the year. But it never was.

I would see close friends, colleagues and cousins with girlfriends and wives, but never me. Often I've wondered if they possessed some kind of magic gene which I was missing, or if I was somehow too different or niche. Time and time again I thought about ditching my hobbies and interests, becoming more 'normal'. Let's face it, from my experience anyway, not many men are interested in poetry, baking, classic literature, classical music and musical theatre. Especially here in Enfield.

Enfield, the land that God forgot. A rancid little armpit of North London where culture goes to die. It's fitting that neighbouring Edmonton shares its name with Chris Benoit's hometown, because I imagine that anyone who passes through there ends up wanting to hang themselves. Yes, that was a wrestling reference. Yet another thing that marks me out as being endearingly niche. I'm still waiting for the endearing part to kick in.

This town of Enfield is where I work and have done since graduating from university eight years ago. I work for a company called Regal Logistics UK & Ireland, a division of the multi-billion-dollar global conglomerate Regal Worldwide Group. In a single-storey business park development right next to a train station which we share with Asda. Not quite the opulent glitz and glamour that I dreamed of during the halcyon days of university.

It was after university that I landed here. Graduated in July with a 1st in Accounting & Finance with Spanish from the University of Greenwich. Started work in August as a Graduate Management Accountant, the first hire by the new Financial Controller into the company's fledgling Finance department. My boss was a lovely Sri Lankan man named Dev who really took me under his wing.

When I started at Regal I was waiting on a call-back from a second interview with JP Morgan. Their beautiful offices were a stone's throw from the Waitrose where I worked at the time. That part-time job saw me through one year of college and three years of university. A few days later the call came and I was offered the Junior Analyst role. And I turned it down, something I've regretted ever since.

So many times I've wondered how different my life would have been if I'd taken that job. I have a cousin who works for Goldman Sachs in Hong Kong and his life is a bubble of constant excitement. Instead of corporate seats at Stamford Bridge and trips to New York, I get Tastecards and discounts at places I never go. I haven't seen a bonus since my last year at Waitrose.

For all of the non-existent excitement, it hasn't all been bad. I qualified as an accountant at 24, three years after graduation, following consecutive first-time exam passes. Upon qualification, I was immediately promoted to Management Accountant, a job I've held ever since. The last five years have been a whirlwind of 3% annual pay increases and trips to exotic hotspots like Ruislip and Birmingham.

I currently make £58,000 a year, not bad at all for a single man living in London. More than enough to keep me in books, and solo trips to the theatre and cinema. Not to mention poetry, my biggest indulgence of all.

Almost four years ago I began to reconnect with my creative side, something which had been dormant since I was 16. This was prompted by a conversation at a bar in Islington with Andre, my best friend since my second day at university. He always tells me that he likes the way I describe things, the way I tell stories, the words, and expressions that I use.

I first discovered poetry at the age of five through Michael Rosen. I'll never forget *Chocolate Cake*. Since then I've always had a great love of reading and writing the poetic form. I guess it's in my blood. At the age of fourteen my head was turned by a field trip to Deutsche Bank, and I left behind any aspirations I had relating to journalism and creative writing. From that day forward I was all about that money.

That said, I continued to excel academically in those more creative arenas. Scored A*-graded GCSEs in English Language, English Literature and Drama, along with three more A*s, two As and three Bs. Achieved 100% for a paper I wrote about *The Crucible* and again for a collection of love poems which were included in the school's GCSE syllabus the year after I left. After that the poetry died.

Next came college and A-Levels. Accounting, Business Studies, Economics and Maths. Nothing creative and all geared towards the career path which I was looking to cultivate. Straight As and my pick of the universities. In the end I chose Greenwich because it meant that I could live at home, something which I did until I was twenty-five, and I wouldn't have to give up my stock control job at Waitrose.

I got back into poetry largely as a means to numb the monotony of work. After writing consistently for a little while, I discovered The Poetry Café in Covent Garden. *Poetry Unplugged* became my sanctuary and every Tuesday night I couldn't wait to get behind the mic. I felt like a star and as though I was among kin. Every week without fail I would ride that adrenaline high right through to the start of work on Wednesday morning, when I would once again feel like an outcast and a weirdo.

None of this poetry or literature stuff made me cool or a hit with the ladies. Shock horror! I grew up on a rough council estate and attended an equally rowdy school. Wasn't very popular, but I always found solace in academia and the promise of a better tomorrow. Rather shockingly, I'm not in touch with Danny Ball, the boy from across the street who once defecated on himself in the school library (on purpose!) or Tammy Arnold, the girl from school who used to call me ugly and in adulthood shacked up with a Cockney Dexter Morgan wannabe (The Bay Harbour Botcher) who decapitated his own sister and dumped her torso in the canal.

It wasn't until university that I truly found my tribe. Met two of my best friends there and met the rest of them through Andre. When I'm with them I feel like I'm somebody and part of something. Anything is possible with The Tiger Pack, and I mean anything. The seven of us took this Stateside road trip to celebrate Andre's 30th, and this trip couldn't have come at a better time for me.

For months beforehand I felt like a jaded shadow of myself, or at least of the new version of myself which had started to blossom for a few months. No longer the office joker but rather a cynical and anti-social old grunt. For all my disappointment at the fact that work wasn't what I dreamed of, I made the best of it after a certain point. At this time, I didn't feel the same way. Gone was the party boy who opened up the Christmas bash with a word-perfect rendition of *Ice Ice Baby* (without looking at the lyrics on the screen!). In his place is this miserable old git.

Just over a year ago I was a shoo-in for a career-making promotion. Our Managing Director, Stephen Cruller, got promoted to the global board while our Finance Director and Dev's boss, Barry Tennyson, took Stephen's old job. Dev was set to become Finance Director with me stepping up and into the Financial Controller position. But everything changed and, in the end, I never got that promotion.

Barry decided to have his cake and eat it by keeping both jobs. Changed the titles to CEO and CFO before making Dev redundant and hiring a new Finance Director in his place. And in he breezed. Hurricane Raj.

Raj Panesar, an Indian man with a penchant for bad wigs which even Burt Reynolds would have rejected. Not that there's anything wrong with that. He also has a huge black hole where most people possess humility, empathy, and social skills. I won't attempt to mitigate that with a *Seinfeld* reference. This man is just the absolute worst. No hyperbole. No exaggeration. And a thief to boot.

Within a matter of months of Raj arriving over half of the department's staff had quit. The complaints against him came thick and fast, yet somehow amid the chaos he ended up getting promoted to COO. This left me having to do the job that he was brought in to do, without the title, glory or money. He kept all of those, taking all the credit while I did the heavy lifting.

The eight months before this trip were undoubtedly the worst of my life. A monolith of days and weeks that existed as the most jarring of blurred fogs, a prolonged concussed stated after colliding head-on with a glass ceiling. That thick and transparent pane cruelly teased me with images of what could have been. More and more I thought about how my life would have turned out if I'd taken the JP Morgan job at 21.

Each passing week saw me become increasingly withdrawn. The frequent out-of-hours working was galling and robbed me of the jovial buzz which I used to bring to my safe, stifling and boring job. Raj would often call me and wake me up on my annual leave days and WhatsApp me on Sundays to work on things which fell under his remit. I was well and truly fed up.

My growing discontent didn't go unnoticed by my peers. I no longer joked around and bantered like I once did and began to grow distant from everyone else. For a few months before this lull, I started to feel like less of an outcast. There was a new girl in Sales, Kelly, with whom I formed something of a friendship. At the same time I was casually flirting with her and angling for something more. The only problem was that everybody wanted her.

Kelly was drawn to my new light, something which Raj set out to dim. Once he forced out Ben, another Management Accountant, he set his sights on me. Took my new-found ebullience for overconfidence and even told me as much. After that, albeit not immediately, I decided to pull the wings off my nascent social butterfly. This, of course, came after he piggybacked off my hard work to reap the kudos for turning around a department which was already facing the right way and acrimoniously usurped a COO who had done nothing but champion him.

Raj got drunk on his growing power and like the very worst of drunks he doled out severe punishment to everyone around him. Changed the daily start time from 9:00 to 8:30 and cut everyone's lunch break to just 30 minutes, whilst not increasing salaries one iota. Cancelled scheduled holidays on a whim. Took himself to the pub in the middle of crucial meetings and expected you to be there when he returned two hours later. Your work and his done, of course. Every day I was swimming against the tide with no dry land in sight.

So joyless was I that I nearly withdrew from this trip, the one thing I was hanging on for. This was after I'd paid for my flights. I just did not care anymore. At the time I told Andre I would be there in spirit. A clear lie. I was finding it hard enough to be where I actually was in spirit, let alone somewhere else. It wasn't until a particularly enjoyable house party with the boys less than a fortnight before the trip that I decided to go and felt pumped about it again.

One wild night of music, drinking, Cards Against Humanity and hurdling over bin bags reduced a multi-month nightmare to a minor irritation and served as a harbinger of the fun to come. Sure, I'd been and old curmudgeon for a few months. Given my nearest and dearest a hard time. Treated the people around me like crap, with Kelly getting the worst of it after we'd grown pretty close. Whined and complained incessantly as Raj went about his quest to outsource every last paperclip in the company to India.

But that was then. This was now. I was ready for the big ride. Ready to fly to the States and have a rollicking good time once I got there, finding something I never knew I was looking for along the way.

Nothing was ever going to be the same again.

CHAPTER 3

Sapphires strip club. Four in the morning. The blue lights are burning hard through an invisible fog of whiskey, marijuana, and musk. Pungent yet not entirely unpleasant permeations stick to the air while ear-splitting hip-hop blasts out in all directions. The club is packed from wall to wall with bodies both clothed and unclothed. Crisp dollar bills are changing hands left and right as a big screen on the back wall shoots a flurry of colours into the self-contained darkness.

I sit comfortably slouched in a leather tub chair, transfixed by the bronze and athletic curves of the exotic beauty before me. She's firmly mounted to the chair while teasingly wearing my new cowboy hat, thrusting hard and fast to the music as my hands clutch her hips. My fingers gently graze the thin material of her lime green thong on both sides. She is wearing nothing but this and her exaggerated heels. And, of course, my hat.

Her long dark hair glides like a magnet following her torso move for move. My hands slide upwards and make a rough grab for her supple breasts before squeezing. Moments later my transient Aphrodite reciprocates by placing her palms over my hands and aiding them in a prolonged squeeze. After she relinquishes, I slink my left hand onto her right hip and move in closer with my right hand still on her left breast. She quickly tilts her head back before my mouth engulfs the erect nipple.

I repeat this ritual on the opposite side while drinking in the sweet scent of her perfume. The track plays on for another minute or so, her grinding picking up and dropping speed in proportion to the embellished electronic beat. Once the music stops, she slowly dismounts, placing a small kiss on my lips and planting my cowboy hat back on my head.

'Thank you, baby.'

'Thank you, Jay.' I grab her breasts again and pull each one into my mouth in turn. I let go and Jay reaches towards the floor before slinking her lime green dress back on over her lithe olive-skinned body. All the while my eyes stay fixed on her as she puts on a little show with this simple action. I stand up once she's dressed.

'Here you go' I say while coolly sliding a $20 bill into the right breast of her dress with my right hand. 'And a little something extra for you.' I tuck a $5 tip into the opposite breast. 'Aww, you're sweet.' She looks at me with her daring brown eyes, a sensual glint with a whiff of mischief escapes. 'So, d'you wanna go private?'

'Ah, I've spent enough time in that private room tonight. Maybe a little too much. But why don't you come back with me to the bar and meet my friends? They will absolutely love you.' While saying this I point towards three suited men of Indian appearance bantering and laughing by the bar, drawing Jay's gaze in the same direction. 'OK, cool. Sounds good.' 'Let's go' I reply with a vigour.

I lead Jay from the centre of the floor towards the bar with my right arm wrapped around her waist. Along the way we continue the laughing and flirting. We stop in front of the bar and catch my three friends chatting and laughing, drinks in hand. Their conversation gently comes to a halt once they notice us in front of them.

'Alright lads. How we doing?' My three friends look on in awe of Jay's Mexican movie star looks while I quietly hold court. 'Hey Michael, you hound dog! Loving the blue suede shoes!' replies Carl, a diminutive gentleman with smooth, clear skin and short black hair sporting a lightly-gelled finish. 'Just don't step on them uh-huh-huh!' I lightly fire back before we break into a symphony of friendly laughter.

'Boys, this is Jay. Jay, this is Carl, Pro and Kam' I say while gesturing from left to right. 'Hey boys, nice to meet you. Y'all having a good time tonight?' 'Oh yeah, definitely' replies Carl. 'He looks like he's having fun!'

he glibly adds while nodding towards me and gently pointing with the glass in his right hand.

'He sure is. Look at what I've done to him!' As Jay says this she points to the bulge in my trousers, prompting laughter from my friends, before grabbing it. 'Well, can you blame me? I mean look at these!' I reply while squeezing each of Jay's breasts with my right hand. This causes both Jay and my friends to laugh in response. 'They're beautiful!' I grab Jay's behind as the laughter continues. After a brief pause, I point and draw her attention to Kam, a tall bald man with glasses holding a glass of Grey Goose vodka in his left hand.

'My friend here has been a very bad boy and he needs to be punished. I reckon you should punish him by burying his face in these.' I grab Jay's breasts again and look across to Kam with a hint of expectation. 'Kam, how many dances have you had so far?' 'None' he replies between slow deliberate sips of vodka. 'Come on Kam. It's time for you to get off the bench and into the game. Whaddya say?'

'Nah mate. I'm alright here.' 'Oh Kam. You don't want to miss out on all of this. I can promise you a really good time. This is the best offer you're going to get all night. Come on everyone! Kam, Kam, Kam, Kam….' Carl and Pro join in the jovial chanting, which goes on for another fifteen seconds or so and ends once Kam throws back the last of his vodka before pounding the empty glass down on the bar.

'Alright. I'm in.' Pro and Carl let out a big cheer while Jay laughs. Kam moves towards Jay and as she leaves my grasp, I slap her on the backside with my right hand. 'Have fun you two. Don't do anything I wouldn't do!' Kam puts his arm around Jay and they head towards the floor. Before they go, I give Jay's backside one last short hard smack.

'Oh my God Michael! That was amazing!' exclaims Pro with a real buzz. 'You're a pimp Michael, a proper pimp!' Carl chimes in with a smile while preparing for a long sip of his drink. 'What went down just now was legend….WAIT FOR IT!....DARY!

I'm abruptly awoken by a hard rapid knock on the door of my hotel room. It's the middle of the day and I haven't slept for longer than a few minutes at a time since waking up yesterday. More than 24 hours have passed and I'm wired hard, the euphoria from last night and this morning running wild and making a whisper of the latently creeping fatigue. Slightly flustered, I tentatively roll off the bed and head for the door.

I open the door and Andre is right there as planned, wearing garishly coloured shorts and an equally bright T-shirt which makes it obvious that he's a tourist. 'Alright Andre. Come in mate.' I close the door behind him and we head towards the beds, where we sit down next to one another. 'How's your eye now?'

'Yeah, it's a little better, thanks. I put some drops in earlier and it seems to be clearing up now.' He tells me this with a smile of quiet relief. 'What do you think caused it?' 'I don't know for sure, but I reckon it was that Cuban girl in the VIP when she was grinding all up on me. Her perfume.'

'Kelly from the office had the same kind of infection. Remember a few weeks ago when I gave her first aid treatment?

'Oh yeah. I remember.'

'Not the same root cause, at least I don't think so, but definitely the same kind of infection.' We break into a short burst of laughter at this, started by Andre.

'Hey Mike, I got your message a few hours ago. You said that you had something crazy to tell me. What is it?'

Andre and I are sitting on high chairs in the food court of the Fashion Show Mall, eating tacos purchased from a Chinese-run Mexican food establishment in the foreground. Chatting and laughing all the way, we are two best friends in tremendous spirits thoroughly enjoying ourselves and one another's company. I take a voracious bite out of a taco, leaving cheese and sauce dripping out of the other end while Andre continues to laugh at my story.

'Geez, I can't believe what happened! Ha ha ha! So, Paresh was lying in bed the whole time you were in there with Lola! Wow! It would have been so funny if he'd walked in!' Andre, half-eaten taco in hand, takes a sip from his soda cup in between chuckles. 'Thankfully, I remembered to lock the door, but I'm pretty sure he heard everything. Lola didn't have any music with her, so she came up with the idea to run the shower so that the water would cover our noise. I'm not sure how much good it did though.' The laughter continues with Andre still incredulous.

'I really hope he didn't hear any of the dialogue. Oh my God, I'll be so embarrassed if he has. I'll have to talk to him later on to find out exactly what he heard.' Andre leans in, curious. 'Why? What exactly did you guys say in there? You've got me interested now. Come on Mike, you've gotta tell me!'

'Alright, I'm lying on the bathroom floor and Lola's on top of me. She's wearing this very cowboy hat and literally nothing else. I started telling her about how we used to have Page 3 girls back home. She was like 'What? You had topless women in your newspapers?' Lola couldn't believe it. Anyway, I said to Lol, no word of a lie, 'If I opened up the newspaper and saw you on Page 3, I'd shoot my load all over that page!'

Andre, even more incredulous than before, roars with raucous laughter in response. 'You said that to her? Wow! That's unbelievable! What did she say to that?' Michael takes another sip of soda before responding. 'She leaned in over me and gave me this playful little slap, a really soft one. Then she said 'Oooh, you nasty!' Michael and Andre share another hearty laugh following this anecdote.

I'm now referring to Michael in third person. But why? Just moments later the old Michael, the old me, would be no more. I ceased being the insecure doormat I once was and the morose, skulking me of the past several months receded into memory's ether. As I recalled the details of my outlandish story, I began reliving it in my mind, moment by moment. It felt good, so very good. I had no idea who this person was. But I liked him. Lola in that bathroom this morning was my *Shirley Valentine* moment, permanently pulling me from the funk that had plagued me for so many months and carving a piece of Vegas into my soul that would stay with me forever.

'Oh Mike, it's so good to have you back to your old self. It really is. I remember what you said to me back in Monterey, about how you got everything you needed from this trip before we left San Francisco. Everything after that was bonus rounds.' Michael raised his soda cup to Andre in a toasting manner. 'Yeah, I guess you could say that I've had a bit of a moment out here. Kinda like Stu in *The Hangover*. Speaking of which, did you see all *The Hangover* merchandise back in the hotel? D'you reckon in Bangkok they have loads of stores selling *Hangover 2* merchandise, ha ha?'

'Ha ha. I doubt it.' Michael, with a relaxed smile on his face, slightly adjusts his hat. 'When we were driving out of Big Sur you said that you'd like to do something different with your life. Work-wise, I mean. Something more client-facing, customer-facing. Have you given any more though to that?' Michael, slightly hesitant, finishes his soda before putting the empty cup down on the table.

'Not really. I suppose there is that opening in the Sales team, working for Anne. They always seem to be having fun. But I don't know. There's a small part of me that wants to stay here in Vegas. Find Lola, take her to one of the local chapels, get married so I can stay in the country.'

'What would you do for work out here Mike? Be a blackjack dealer?'

My mind sinks back to Sapphires. The blue light piercing the black immerses me and the errant splinters of lurid colour dapple my face. My mouth is moving but I can't hear myself speak for the mass of ambient noise and memory's lack. Andre is right next to me and spirits are in the sky. The muted laughter goes back and forth as bodies pass in all directions, seemingly in slow-motion. A gentle euphoria is burning slowly inside of me like a well-lit cigar.

The music powders out and I can hear nothing but a grating ringing in my ears. Everything else looks the same while no other sound can escape. With each passing moment the ringing grows louder and envelops me even more. My heart beats like a brick against the inside of my chest, the force contrasted by the silence it leaves in its wake. The ringing catches a static fizz, like a radio being tuned or a lit fuse just before exploding, until all the sounds suddenly collapse into one. Then just like that they faded.

'I could totally run vice in this town!'

Right there and then The Money Man was born.

CHAPTER 4

The Money Man. An egregious moniker earned during my graduate days at Regal while I was developing the company's cash flow forecasting. I had my finger on every penny of a billionaire absentee landlord's money, but never on the things I truly wanted. Too often I was afraid of disappointing others and just did what was expected of me, often to my own detriment. The extra miles I went were taken for granted and only truly noticed whenever I held a couple back.

But no more.

No more will I seek permission and seldom will I seek forgiveness after the fact. I'm a new man who tells rather than asks, tells you what he's going to do while giving no explanation why and not waiting around for your approval. I no longer wonder what others think of me, and nor do I care. This is my way and nobody else's. No other person could walk the road that I forge, so what should I care what they think of how I walk it?

I look around this town and I see a place where anything is possible. Every pocket of flashing neon puncturing a crevice of darkness is like a door on an advent calendar. Behind each one is something I deserve, right there for the taking. The lights are blinding, spellbinding even. I'm staring down this opulently lurid desert pit and I'm determined that the town will blink first.

Now I demand and expect rather than hope. I know who I am, what I am, what I represent and, most importantly, what I'm worth.

Lola and I are sitting on the tiled bathroom floor wearing nothing but smiles, kissing with a joyfully unabashed abandon. I've lost all track of time but I don't care. Nothing matters except for the here and now. The great time she promised me has been had. Right now, I'm feeling something else. Something that goes beyond attraction and mere physical acts. Something real. Something wonderful and unknown to me is about to reveal its face….

Until Lola's beeper goes off!

'Damn!' she exclaims. 'I'm gonna lose my babysitter.'

'You have a kid?' I reply with an air of surprise. 'Yeah. A little girl. Her name's Jennifer. She's four years old.' 'That's lovely' I reply. 'Jennifer is everything to me. I'm so proud of her.' I give a warm and silent smile upon hearing this while reaching into the front pocket of the trousers strewn across the floor behind me. A moment or two later I pull out a brown leather wallet with my right hand. After casually flipping the wallet open with my left hand, I slide out four crisp hundred dollar bills which I coolly pass to Lola.

'Here you go babe' I say while handing Lola the cash. She takes the bills in her right hand and tucks them into her purse. 'Thank you, baby. Do you believe in tipping for good service?' Almost on cue and impressed by Lola's direct approach, I hand over two more C-notes. 'That's sweet' says Lola before kissing me on the lips.

'Why don't I give you my number? Maybe we could get together again before you fly home on Sunday.' Lola's offer brings a big smile to my face. 'You know what? I would love that. Ah, but I don't have a pen.' 'You're so old-fashioned!' Lola blurts with a snicker. 'You can give me your phone and I'll put my number in for you.'

'Sounds good to me.' Keeping my eyes and smile fixed on Lola, I rather clumsily scramble behind my back with my right hand, trying to find my phone. After several seconds of trying and failing to find my phone, lightly cursing under my breath through most of it, I suddenly give up and focus all of my attention on Lola once more.

'I'll find you.'

It's a sweet Nevada autumn night and the weather is high, the wind chilled with thrown caution and discarded inhibitions burning in the desert ether. The seven of us stroll into Treasure Island like a triumphant cavalry returning home, breezing past a series of lively tables, and taking in the assorted whoops and hollers from the games of chance unfolding all around us.

The scene at the bar is dazzling. Picture perfect working girls line the perimeter, enthusiastically touting for business from the jolly drinking men all around them. Pretty faces and designer garments of all shades speckle the foreground with glitz under the golden lights. Single-serving temptation in every other stool.

And there she was. Again.

'So, Mike, which one is Lola?' asks Pro, gently leaning over my right shoulder. 'That's her' I reply, nodding my head and motioning towards Lola as she talks to a burly suited gentleman. She looks immaculate and identical to how she did when I met her this morning with the exception of her top. It's beige and sleeveless like the one she wore before but lined with strips of tinsel-like gold.

'Why don't you go over and say hello?' Andre asks earnestly. 'No way! That's creepy!' The conversation dissipates and I lead the seven-strong charge left towards the restaurant. This eatery is a vast open space behind a brown wooden partition. Diners pack the tables and look on at the non-stop commotion from the bar and casino while enjoying their meals. Each table is signposted by two menus in the centre, one for traditional American food and the other Chinese cuisine. Waiters and waitresses in contrasting attire serving very different dishes co-mingle and roam freely around the space.

'Good evening gentlemen.'

A tall bespectacled waitress in her sixties greets us warmly at the entrance. 'Table for seven please' says Carl. 'Table for seven? Right this way.' The waitress kindly leads us towards four connecting two-seater tables at the front of the establishment. I deliberately seat myself so that I have a clear view of Lola at the bar. She is sitting alone now with a drink in her hand. The gentleman from earlier is nowhere to be seen.

Our waitress pulls out her pad and starts taking drinks orders from our party while I look at the American menu. I spend several seconds fixating on the steak and eggs before the chirpy voice of the waitress beckons me. 'What'll it be young man?' 'O'Doul's please.' She scribbles another quick note with her right hand. 'I'll be right back with your drinks.'

'How hot were those showgirls?' I say, turning to Andre. 'Especially that Ashton. Wow!' 'Oh yeah, just don't go sharing that picture you got with her on your Facebook. I know what you're like!' 'Come on, what's the worst that could happen? Are you worried that old Toupee Shakur is going to see it? Fuck him!'

'You have to be careful with CIMA and everything. They look at the profiles of all their members. You know that.' I take a slow sip of water and then put the glass on the table. 'I know, I know. Anyway, who said I still want to be an accountant?' With a big smile on my face, I raise the glass in my right hand.

I feel a cool sense of peace washing over me, one unlike any I have felt before. No longer burdened by rules, expectations and binary definitions from outside forces, I am both the reinvigorated artist and the blank canvas upon which the new masterpiece will be created. I feel as though I'm standing on the precipice of something I've never know before, something amazing.

'So, tell me, did you throw eggs at his window?'

We're on the steps of Da Poetry Lounge in Los Angeles, laughing and joking with two muscular black bouncers. The conversation moves towards *The Wire* and I end up fielding a truly bizarre question from one of them after I mention that I grew up ten minutes down the road from where Idris Elba did.

'No. I can't say I ever did.'

Over my right shoulder I hear a couple of charming giggles. I turn around and see two pretty young blonde girls, greeting them with a smile. Surprised and enchanted by their presence, I take the opportunity to walk over and greet the young ladies. They're more than happy to receive me and we strike up a rapport right away.

'Hello ladies.'

'Hey.'

'So, are you two here for the slam?'

'Yeah. I'm on the judging panel and my friend here has come along to support me. How about you?'

'I'm going to be performing in the slam, provided we can get in. I'm Michael.'

'I'm Pamela.'

'And I'm Brittany.'

'Nice to meet you ladies. You're both looking rather lovely this evening.' I take a hand of each lady in my right hand and plant a gentlemanly kiss on each one in turn. This makes both Pamela and Brittany gush rather gleefully in response.

'Oh, such a gentleman!' coos Pamela. 'Yes, he is!' Brittany replies enthusiastically. 'Nice to meet you. So, you're going to be performing later on, huh? Do you think we could get a little preview of your poem, just for us? I smile teasingly for a few moments before responding.

'Oh, go on then. Just for you.'

'Great.'

Both ladies smile with anticipation as I prepare to launch into a snap performance, channelling Sir Ian McKellen while placing a hand on one shoulder of each lady.

'Demons fall from the grace of the wicked
Angels gravitate towards the refuge of villainy
Good and evil sit side by side
Like chiral viscous droplets in a Petrie dish
Longing to collide
And form something else entirely
Which is both

But neither
Yet exists as one.'

'Excuse me.'

I abruptly rise from my seat and proceed to leave the restaurant, leaving behind the chatter about cars. A few questions and puzzled looks come my way but those visions and sounds quickly collapse into one. As I saunter towards the bar with a purpose my gaze doesn't leave Lola and the empty barstool next to her. The bartender, Cristobal, spots me as I get closer to the bar and smiles.

'O'Doul's and one for yourself' I tell him.

Lola turns around quickly and greets me with a look of pleasant surprise. I quickly disarm her before she has a chance to speak.

'I have a proposition for you.'

CHAPTER 5

Just another day at the office. The green and white of spreadsheet after spreadsheet engulfs my two screens. Columns upon columns and rows upon rows of nothing but numbers. Profits, losses, margins, variances, percentages, projections, ratios. I read between the lines of every digit and I see myself dying one report at a time.

For a moment I try to fantasize about a life unlike this one but my attempt at quiet reflection is broken up on two fronts. Firstly, by the adjacent cavalcade of obnoxious noise coming from the sewing circle we call Accounts Payable. The brass section, and I mean that in every sense of the word, is led by Velma, a middle-aged Greek-Cypriot woman who's as loud as the day is long and twice as asinine.

Dev really wanted to fire her and most of the rest of her team. That was before Barry took over the line management of Accounts Payable, around the same time it became apparent that he was sleeping with Velma behind his wife's back. And her husband's. Barry lets her and that team get away with murder, mucking about at the expense of the company while leaving the rest of the department to pick up the pieces. He even allowed her to bring in her idiot best friend, who didn't know what GBP was until I told her and can't even write linguistically correct e-mails, to be her supervisor. Barry has a lot to answer for.

The accounts became such a mess as a knock-on effect of their antics. Barry blamed Dev and showed him the door, after Dev and I cleaned up that mess. Often Barry puts a little extra in his little floozy's pay packet. I think there's a name for that. Meanwhile the rest of us have to put up with her bad singing, inane questions ('Is Bangladesh in the EU?') and dull patter. If I hear one more story about the husband who supposedly works security for Alan Sugar, I'll kill myself with my own Post-Its.

He even lets her sell clothes in the office and said 'These things happen' when only my intervention prevented a payment of £2.2 million which she'd wrung up from going through. The supplier in question was owed just £22,000.

Further on the in the foreground I see Raj talking to John, the dutiful jobsworth Treasury Accountant. He's handing John another bogus direct debit mandate from a company owned by one of his friends. John won't question it. He doesn't like confrontations and particularly hates questioning authority. Raj will tell him 'We are in it to win it!' before leaving his desk. I've heard that stupid speech many times. Dale Winton turns in his grave every time.

If he's over there then at least he's not at his desk, which is to the left of mine. As always, his monitor screen is unlocked. No concept of data protection or confidentiality. Everyone but Raj, Barry and Velma gets a £1 fine for that. A £1 fine for leaving your desk with your screen unlocked. Truly a novel policy, courtesy of Regal Records Management General Manager Jim Fathers. Anyone who cares to look can see their bank log-in details.

Right on cue Raj gives that stupid speech. Even tumbleweed doesn't yield when he gets going. A moment of relative silence presents itself and I take a stolen tuft of time to fantasize about a life unlike this one.

I sit opposite Lola at a table in the Treasure Island restaurant, both of us enjoying the breakfast steak and eggs. I've not slept since the early hours of Thursday. It's now Saturday morning and 24 hours have passed since our first encounter at the bar to my right. A happy calm breezes between us as we comfortably share a silence while dining.

'So, what happens now?' I ask between mouthfuls of steak. 'Well, obviously, you're gonna move in with me. That's what married people do. I'm now Alexa Velez-O'Sullivan. The least you can do after saddling me with that hyphen and those extra syllables is move into my apartment.' Lola lets out a jovial laugh as she says this. 'There's plenty of toom and it's a nice building. Nice neighbours.'

'Sounds good to me.'

'Tomorrow. You move in tomorrow. I need to talk to Jennifer, explain things to her. Come over for breakfast. I'll whip us up some of my delicious French toast. I can't wait for you to meet my daughter.'

'I look forward to it.'

'Spend today with your friends. Paint the strip red one last time before they go home. I'm sure they'll want to give you a good send-off.'

'Kam will insist. I know that much.'

'He's a lot of fun. I can't believe he wears an Abercrombie fleece in this heat, ha ha.'

'Yeah, he's an interesting guy. Love Kam. He sure knows how to throw a party.'

'Sounds like it. That story you told me about him trying to hurdle over those garbage bags was so funny.'

'Ha ha ha.'

'What do you boys have planned for today?'

'We're going to see Cirque Du Soleil this evening. At this hotel. Before then I'm planning to get some sleep.'

'That's right, Party Boy. You've been up for two days straight.'

'Yeah, two days. Wow. That false oxygen they pump in here isn't helping. Might I add that I'm now married to the foxiest lady in all of Las Vegas, so I don't see that sleep situation of mine improving anytime soon.' I flash Lola a cheeky wink, bringing a coy smile to her face.

'I want you to have fun tonight, but I also need you nice and fresh for tomorrow, so sleeping now is a good idea. Jennifer's very intellectually curious, so inquisitive. Four going on forty. Great kid. I just hope that you can handle her.'

'She sounds amazing. What happened to her dad?'

'He left before Jennifer was born. Never met her. Since then, it's just been the two of us. No boyfriends, no stepdads. That's all she's ever known.'

'That sounds exactly like my parents.'

'Oh yeah?'

'Yeah. I never knew my dad. It was always mum and I. When I was really young, she worked multiple jobs to provide for us. Nursing, teaching at an adult education centre, childminding, giving English lessons to some of the local Bengali kids. She did it all and made sure I wanted for absolutely nothing. But she always made sure I did my homework first. When I was in secondary school, she got me a big brown wooden desk for my bedroom that's way bigger than the one I now have at work. I wrote many an essay there. It even had a gold lamp on top with a dark green shade. Looked like something right out of the Oval Office.'

'She sounds like an incredible woman. Very strong.'

'Oh yeah, she's formidable. Just like you. A lot of that is immigrant survival instinct. She came over to London when she was just sixteen to be a nurse. Knew nobody, had nobody. It wasn't a great time to be in England either. No blacks, no Irish, no dogs.'

'What?'

'Back then if you tried to rent a room, you'd see countless signs in windows with those very words on. No blacks, no Irish, no dogs.'

'Oh my God. That's terrible.'

'Yeah. What can you do? The funny thing is that she often ended up treating these very same people at her hospital.'

'My folks went through a lot of the same thing. They both came over to New York from Dorado as adults. Mom worked in catering while she studied to improve her English. Dad worked odd jobs, cleaning and such, and Mom supported him while he studied. Eventually he became a CPA, got a Master's degree in IT and worked as an accountant for the government. That was before he got a job as a professor at Carnegie Mellon and moved us all to Pittsburgh.'

'That's impressive.'

'They made me who I am today. Isn't that the old cliché? Well, for better or worse, I suppose they did.'

'Do tell.'

'I definitely inherited their strength, but sometimes the load of having to be that strong all the time us too much to carry. When I was younger, I wanted to be an English teacher, but my folks didn't approve. It didn't have enough prestige for their liking. They had the struggle and they wanted a more comfortable life for me, so they pushed me towards science.'

'Science?'

'Yeah. I was always really good at it, won lots of science awards and fairs in high school, but it wasn't what I wanted to do for a career. It was something I really enjoyed, but like you I was more interested in books, stories and poems. After high school I ended up at Carnegie Mellon. Biomedical and forensic science.'

'Wow. That must have been an interesting course.'

'It was. We even did a module on blood spatter. On our very first day of college, they gave us a crazy exercise. We were all given a shredded document and told to put it back together with tape.'

'That's mental.'

'Not to mention the skulls and bones. Just before spring break in my freshman year I had a mental breakdown. The pressure got to be too much. I ended up dropping out and moving back home.'

'I'm sorry to hear that.'

'It's OK. Honestly. I'm fine now. I decided to take a year off while I figured out what I was going to do next. Started dancing at the local Spearmint Rhino. The money was good. I felt rich. At the end of a slow week I was taking home $1,000. I really liked it. The other girls were really cool and I had some good customers.'

'How did you end up doing that?'

'A friend suggested that I try it. One day during the summer I auditioned and the rest is history.'

'I bet you were really popular with the customers.'

'Sure was. That was the problem.'

'How so?'

'I hit it off really well with this one customer, an investment banker at Morgan Stanley. He was something else.'

'Yeah?'

'Oh yeah. He was a real gentleman. Matt would come to the club to see me and only me. On my nights off I sometimes got called in at the last minute because he showed up asking for me. We always talked and laughed and he was a great tipper. The first night he came to the club we got talking and soon enough he started taking me out to nice hotels, restaurants, plays, ballet. It was all champagne, strawberries, breakfast and movies in bed at first. That was great, I loved it.'

'And then what happened?'

'A few weeks before Christmas I found out that I was pregnant. I called Matt right away and he offered to meet me for breakfast the next morning so that we could talk. He never showed and I never heard from him again. Matt Mitchell blocked and ghosted me at every turn. He called my boss at the club and told him what happened. That day I lost everything.'

'He sounds like a really nasty piece of work. What kind of person does that to another human being?'

'I know, right? In that moment I was nineteen, pregnant, jobless, and homeless. My parents turfed me out once I told them the news. They told me to sort my life out and recognise that I was a screw-up. I didn't talk to them for a while after that. Their words hit me really hard but at the same time I was determined to make good on what they said to me. Pretty early on into the pregnancy I decided that I was going to keep my baby.'

'Good for you. Clearly you did the right thing. It must have been really tough though, being out on your own and with child like that. You should be very proud of yourself. I'm very proud of you.'

Lola quietly smiles and slides her right hand across the table in a gentle manner softly squeezing my left hand while looking at me lovingly. I return her warm gaze and before long I am gleefully lost in the rapture of our tender moment. This is a whirlwind of genuine, honest affection which neither of us saw coming.

'I wasn't alone alone. My girls from the club had my back. I even moved in with one of them, a sweet

Filipina girl named Gemma, before I got an apartment of my own. Once I got settled, I started to think about how I was going to provide for my child. Gemma helped me to get a job in another local club and I began escorting as well. Stripping is a great way to meet the clients. I also decided to study for my real estate license, which I now have.'

'Real estate? So, you want to sell houses?'

'I'm thinking long-term. I want to invest and develop. Not planning to be stripping and escorting forever. This is just a stop gap. I'm saving my money. Every week I save at least $100. Five years from now I want to be out of this racket and fully up and running in real estate.'

'That's why this opportunity we have is absolutely perfect.'

'Let's not talk about it here. We can go up to the room once we've finished up.'

'Sure.'

CHAPTER 6

Another long train ride to work. Four trains and an hour and a half to get me to my destination, my crack den where I load up on my daily fix of disappointment and tedium. I embrace the occasional delays to my journey. They allow me to steal a few extra minutes to myself, time spent away from the banal squawking that will permeate the atmosphere once I arrive.

I'm just one Good News Friday away from snapping. Ah yes, Good News Friday. Another woefully infantile innovation from our HR department. Once a quarter we meet in the kitchen and form a circle before each sharing a recent piece of good news. It's even more facile than it sounds.

I always imagined team-building activities that involved fancy bars, restaurants and clubs, witty conversation, and a generous company tab. This is so far removed from all of that in the most tragically comic way possible. The only true Good News Friday will be the one that sees me belt out a rendition of *Take This Job & Shove It*.

These extra few minutes give me time to read, to write, to think and sometimes to sleep. But most importantly they give me time to forget. To forget the nagging issues from the day before and temporarily cease anticipating the new headaches that will cling to them during the day ahead. While I forget I think of what might have been and what could still be.

We're all alone now in the hotel room I've been sharing with Paresh since Wednesday. Two heads on a pillow and not another sound to be heard. This is a warm and peaceful haven of our own creation, completely at odds with the frenetic circus of colours that booms beyond our doors and windows. The mood is all business but the love lingers on.

'I work for myself. I'm my own boss and always have been as far as escorting is concerned. The other girls who work this patch answer to Raven Garcia, a local pimp and would-be hustler.'

'Would-be?'

'Yeah. He's always trying to come up in the drug game, but he's really just a cowboy. A rip and run artist who's always stepping on the wrong toes. He works in a courier capacity for this big Jewish gangster and is trying to come up as a distributor himself. The girls all stay in this one house, not his. Nile, his trap queen of a boyfriend, stays there a few nights a week and watches over them.'

'How do you know all this?'

'I'm friends with the girls. We talk a lot. Sometimes I give them rides home after work.'

'Aren't you the competition?'

'Technically I am. I've done really well here so far, particularly with tips. Raven takes all their money anyway, so there's no beef with me. On nights when any of them are short I give them some extra cash so they don't cop a beating later on.'

'A beating?'

'Yeah. So many times, I've seen them go to work with poorly concealed bruises. They make no money because of the bruises and then they get beaten again because they've made no money.'

'He sounds like a nasty piece of work.'

'Indeed.'

'First thing Monday working we go to the bank and then Western Union. From the numbers we've talked about half of our savings should do it. Throw in his 10% mailbox money from our take and he's got himself a pretty sweet deal.'

'That's six figures for just walking to the mailbox.'

'It's quite the deal.'

'Do you think he'll bite?'

'I do. He's up to his eyeballs in debt and in way over his head with the gangs around here, especially the bikers. That's why he's trying to distribute drugs on his own. He's always getting high on his own supply and breaking promises made to people who break bones.'

'Wow.'

'Yeah. He needs this.'

'So, what happens after we make the deal with Raven?'

'We start recruiting. Open our accounts, open up our business, spend a week or so getting our affairs in order and then we start up the week after next.'

'That's fast.'

'You wanted to do this, so we're doing it.'

'Look at you!'

'Yeah, well, no time like the present. From what you told me about JP Morgan and everything, you've spent a lot of time talking about things that never get done. You were impulsive enough to drag me off to a chapel and marry me on the day you met me. I want to see some more of that bravery. Besides, Michael, do you have anything better to do in that time?'

'I'm due back at work on Thursday. I suppose I better call my boss and tell him what to do with his crappy job.'

'That will be fun. Don't forget to mention his awful wig.'

'Ha ha.'

'Before we get up and running, we've got to do something for Raven's girls.'

'How do you mean?'

'They've endured years of abuse and will need help starting over, whether they stay on with us or not. We can take care of them, get them back on track. Call it CSR.'

'I like it. You've got such a big heart.'

'My experience of this game was very different from theirs. I do this because I like it and I've been very fortunate.'

'Just because you like it?'

'The money's always been good. Stripping made it easy for me to meet clients and make big money fast. Luckily for me I do like the work, largely because I work for myself, make my own schedule and set my own prices. My clients have always treated me very well.'

'I don't know what to say.'

'People in this line of work deserve to be treated with the same dignity as anyone else.'

'You're so right Lola. I couldn't agree more.'

'Once we're up and running we're going to take good care of our girls. I'm talking about private medical insurance, dental cover, non-contributory pension plans, the whole nine yards. All of our girls will be independent contractors, working for themselves. That's the way it should be.'

'You've really given it some thought.'

'I thought about what my experience was and also what it wasn't. What I had was great but I didn't have everything. You've obviously thought a lot about the money side of things.'

'What can I say? It's in my blood.'

'Ever the accountant.'

'Our revenue model would bring us $7.2 million a year as a headline number and $3.6 million in gross profit. I need to crunch the admin expense numbers but, I have to say, it all looks very promising. Very promising indeed.'

'So, this time next year we'll be millionaires?'

'Ha ha.'

'What is it?'

'There was a comedy series back home called *Only Fools & Horses*. It was about these two brothers, Del Boy and Rodney….'

'Del Boy?'

'Yeah. Well, Derek, but everyone called him Del Boy. They were market traders.'

'The stock market?'

'No no. They had a market stall. Street vendors. They used to sell all kinds of junk, most of it stolen. Anyway, Del always used to say 'This time next year we'll be millionaires'. He would say that in almost every episode.'

'You must show it to me.'

'Consider it done.'

'So, this time next year we'll be millionaires?'

'Again, consider it done.'

It's around 9:30 in the morning on the second Tuesday in February. I have a savant-like ability to recall useless minutiae like that which has long made me suspect that I'm somewhere on the autism spectrum. Months from now I will likely be able to remember those details before any other aspect of this story.

Just another boring day at the office. The same old faces and voices. A bubble of tedium seemingly impervious to the outside rebel forces of excitement. On this day an errant mortar flew across the sky and grazed the bubble's outer shell, flashing a tenuous fire of something mildly interesting.

The police are here. Three officers in full unform. Two male, one female. I've seen a lot of things here, but never this. The whole office is watching. Everyone looks on curiously as the three officers head towards the back of the office before stopping suddenly by Velma's desk.

Yes, her again. Barry is at her desk and they're discussing something completely unrelated to work. The cops figure that he looks official, must be in charge, so they decide to talk to him. He initially seems surprised and annoyed in equal measure. It must have broken his heart to tear himself away from his mistress and their riveting conversation about quantum mechanics.

I listen in while typing away. Or at least I try to. Raj is sat to my left, conducting business on his phone. He complains about a 'Typical Bengali' tenant. After noticing the cops, he rather nervously and abruptly ends the conversation before heading towards the cops. Once again, his monitor is unlocked.

It turns out that Velma 'accidentally' knocked the receiver off her desk phone and accidentally called 999. The dispatcher heard heavy breathing and decided to send a unit over. What a crock of shit. Barry buys it, but he really doesn't. This woman gets away with so much. Anyone else would have been shown the door if they had made as many duplicate supplier payments as Velma and her two idiot friends, Remziye, who is also her boss, and Cenay.

I shake my head watching this unfold while imagining the cops walking Raj out of the building to a massive round of applause.

CHAPTER 7

I find myself alone and bathing in the aftermath of
euphoria during the burgeoning hours of Sunday
morning. A time when everywhere else the wheel
stops, allowing the spokes some much-needed time to
repair and reflect, but here the gears turn harder than
ever. The bright lights of casinos pierce the still noir
with a lullaby of decadence and debauchery.

My own night served up both of these things in
abundance. Lola was right. Kam did insist of throwing
me a killer stag party, after she insisted to him that he
do just that. And what a party it was, a truly glorious
last blast from my old permanently single life in
London and into a brave new world of marriage,
(step)fatherhood, Vegas and vice.

As I walk back through the strip, south to north, a
kaleidoscope of raucous memories pushes a happy
tear out of my right eye. The tear slowly rolls down
along my face as I take in the lurid glory all around me.
I look around at the here and now while my thoughts
switch between the past, present and future.

In terms of send-offs, tonight was pretty much perfect.
Sleep ended up being impossible after Lola left my
room, so I spent the day roaming the strip by myself.
Rode the High Roller, bought some gifts for Mum and
friends back home, talked football with some friendly

locals who noticed my Messi jersey and got plenty of photos. The best was one of me being arrested by two attractive young ladies in skimpy rent-a-cop outfits.

When I got back to my room for another attempt at sleep, I found a note from Kam posted under my door. It read to meet him and the rest of the boys at Starbucks outside the hotel at 6pm. I found that very strange considering that we were planning to see Cirque Du Soleil at the theatre in our hotel at six but I thought nothing more of it.

I stepped outside the hotel at exactly five minutes to six. The boys are standing outside Starbucks engaged in conversation. As I approach Kam turns around and signals to somebody on his left using the index finger on his right hand. Almost on cue a horn loudly honks, drawing my attention to a double-decker bus with tinted windows. Our ride for the evening.

The next several hours were an absolute bacchanal of the most outrageous variety. We did a lap of the strip from north to south before turning back for the reverse lap once we passed Mandalay Bay and the MGM Grand. Spirits were high and in the red solo cups as loud music pumped, Cuban cigars burned and alcohol, or O'Doul's in the case of myself, Pro and Waqas, flowed.

Upon arriving at the Encore, the music stops and the doors of the party bus swing open. Three women in long black trench coats board the bus to a chorus of cheers. Leading the way is a petite dark-skinned beauty with athletic curves and a pretty face bearing an intriguing combination of South Asian and European features. Behind her are two white women with striking Mediterranean looks, one taller and more voluptuous and the other slenderer yet still impossibly buxom.

The next few hours are a delightful blur of sheer hedonism. This mark on my neck is a gleeful reminder of a truly amazing night. Our bus did a few more laps of the famed Las Vegas Strip while our trio of delectable strippers put on quite the show. Kam, ever the party planner, brought a plentiful supply of baby oil, whipped cream and chocolate sauce, all of which came into play on board the bus. That veritable sundae was applied by and to me at different points in time.

The highlight of the bus ride, apart from eating ridiculous amounts of whipped cream off the enormous breasts of Gabriella, the big-bottomed Brazilian stripper, involved me being stripped naked by the girls, tied by my neck to a pole with a leather leash and playfully whipped as my best friends looked on and laughed. I remember feeling really happy when they untied me and Pantera, the sultry Eurasian, sprayed whipped cream on my crotch. My boys truly are the best and I will miss them all dearly.

Just before half then the bus pulled in at the MGM Grand for Kam's next surprise. Lil' Jon live at Hakassan. We sang along to all the hits, waved our arms from the window to the wall, got drenched in the star attraction's sprayed champagne and handed out his complimentary shots amongst ourselves. Before we left, I did something which I've always wanted to do. I bought a $500 bottle of champagne and jubilantly soaked my boys in the bottle's golden fizzing nectar. It made me feel like Lewis Hamilton up on the podium.

After leaving Hakassan, we headed for the Aria. Andre, Carl and I jaywalked to the other side of the Strip and climbed over a hedge to get to the Aria, while the rest of the group sensibly crossed the road at the lights. At this precise moment I was a picture of relaxed joy, buzzing yet content at the same time.

Hedge and all, the three of us made it to the Aria before Kam, Pro, Waqas and Paresh. By the time they reached the blackjack table I was on a real heater, Carl and Andre either side of me cheering me on and enjoying free drinks being served by a pretty Chinese hostess. The dealer flips over two cards to reveal a king of diamonds and a ten of spades. I signal to him that

I'm out before taking my $235 of chips, won on a $60 stake, off the table and leaving.

The mood was jubilant on the way to the cash desk. As we walk past the sports book, I recall how Tony Soprano fell for this old trick and lost all of his winnings on a horse before he could even cash them in. This brought a knowing smile to my face. I looked at my boys with a sense of pride, gratitude and, ultimately, sadness at how much I would miss them.

Our long walk back to Treasure Island was truly magical. Ebullient LCD screens swished light of many colours into the jasmine-scented sky while the fountain at the Bellagio glided seamlessly against the moist night air. We bundle past a cavalcade of clackers handing out business cards for strippers and hookers and a bearded beggar holding up a rather unique cardboard placard, asking for spare change to go towards his penis extension.

Back at the Treasure Island bar everyone is fixing for a nightcap. Kam's vodka Martini, shaken not stirred, is a disappointment in a plastic cup and the usual working girls are nowhere to be seen. I buy an ice-cold O'Doul's and tell Cristobal, the Filipino bartender, to keep the change from the $20 bill. The drinks have barely been sipped by the time Kam suggests one last hurrah.

Half an hour later and Kam and I are in Spearmint Rhino while the rest of our boys are in bed. After a quick round of drinks, we separate and I find myself being entertained in the VIP area by Candy, a perfect brick-built ebony Aphrodite with sumptuous jet-black size 14 curves. I gleefully offer no resistance as a naked Candy grinds her bountiful backside into my crotch and thrusts her enormous breasts into my face. In the distance I see Kam at the bar sipping an old fashioned while talking to two blonde dancers.

After a few hours I'm outside the club on my own. I can't find Kam for the life of me. I get his voicemail three times before giving up and leaving a message in the WhatsApp group chat for everyone to meet me at the bar in a couple of hours. We initially agreed to meet later than that for a breakfast drink of sorts before Kam and I headed to Spearmint Rhino, but I've changed my mind now. I want to surprise my beautiful new wife with breakfast in bed. The thought conjures memories of Joe Pesci in *Casino*, coming home to make breakfast for his young son after a long night heisting diamonds.

I walk laps of the vaunted Strip with a cheery tear in my eye, thinking about the hard goodbye to come. Memories of the rowdy house party from January with Andre, Kam, Tim, Alina, Pravin and Siva, the night when Andre convinced me to come on this trip, come flooding back in abundance. They mesh with the wild memories we made tonight as a strange sense of peace envelops me.

With each step towards Treasure Island, I'm moving further away from my old life towards an unknown that's equal parts terrifying and exhilarating. The darkest of the night imbues a million promises behind the veil of a full, fat moon. Promises of a gleaming new dawn. One unlike all those that came before it only to usher in the same day again and again.

The future looms large and I can't wait for daylight to come.

It's the second Saturday in May. The streets are deserted and I don't recognise them in the slightest. I boarded the wrong night bus and took a turn, ending up somewhere around Crystal Palace scrambling to find the nearest train station. I'm lost and longing to feel the bed under my back. A couple of hours sleep, however tenuous, before going out again.

Another night out with the work clan has come and gone. Yet another one which started and ended with me on my own. Fun was had, promises of even greater exploits were made by the night and ultimately broken by the cruel morning. Most of the night was spent on the terrace of Babble City in Liverpool Street with regular trips to the dancefloor.

Most of our group went home early, leaving myself, Jason from Credit Control and Aaron from IT as the last men standing (and I the lone man sober). Aaron and Jason's antics grew more ridiculous with each passing drink. At one point Aaron began complaining about his pay to some strangers while Jason tried and failed to impress a Bulgarian man in return for free drinks. His chosen party trick involved him putting out cigarettes on his bare palm.

After leaving the club around five we head towards Shoreditch looking for some strip club action. As we prepare to head into a grotty, dimly-lit establishment, I'm propositioned by a dishevelled, coked-up hooker with scraggy blonde hair. I reject her advances while walking away past the bombastic overtures of a would-be pimp who is actually a bouncer. He offers to drive us to a house packed with hot women but we decline. This man must really hate his life.

Aaron hails a cab and leads us to a 24-hour strip club in Holborn. We get there 15 minutes later to find it closed before parting ways. This served as a fitting and stinging metaphor for not only the night but for my life as a whole. It was fun but once again I'm going home alone and tired. Next time, I vow. Next time.

This is the latest in a flurry of nights like that, followed by mornings like this. I always relish the debuting daylight of such a morning, and today is no exception. For the first time, though, it all feels just a little less joyful than all the previous occasions.

I'm happy enough but Monday will come around again fast. Something is missing. I don't quite know what but I hope to find it in Vegas come October.

CHAPTER 8

As Lola parks up the Station Wagon we eye up a gaudy pink two-storey house over on our right. The morning sun does this monstrosity no favours, and the apology for a car parked outside even less. A phosphorescent white SUV with egregiously cheesy gold rims, an unapologetic and crass symbol of dirty money if ever there was one. Standing guard outside the front door is a robust black man with a bald head and granite expression, the tail of his long black trench coat teasing the concrete beneath him.

'If I'm not out in fifteen minutes, something's wrong.' I gently kiss Lola on the lips before leaving the car. As the door on the passenger side slams shut behind me, I walk around the back of the car and stop for a moment to further survey the house. While I look across the road at the garish abode the bouncer's gaze and frame don't move an inch. Yet somehow, he seems alert to my presence and intentions.

After taking a deep breath I tentatively inch towards the house. With each passing step my heart wells up with a heavy air of trepidation. My eyes remain fixed on the bouncer as the emphatic steps try in vain to silence my rapid heartbeat. He remains stoic and still as I close in on him, as though he's waiting for me to blink first.

'Can I help you?'

'I'm here to see Raven.'

'What business could you possibly have here, boy scout?'

'Treasure Island.'

'Shit!'

'No, just Treasure Island.'

'Funny. You got any more of them jokes, boy scout?'

'No, but I do have a proposition for Raven.'

'How do you know about Treasure Island?'

'It's a small world.'

'Stick your arms out.'

'What?'

'Not a request. I'm patting you down.'

'This is ridiculous.'

'Price of admission. I need to know that you're not a cop.'

'I'm from London.'

'Listen, Harry Styles, I don't care where you're from. You're up in here saying you've got business for Raven and I've never seen you before. If you wanna see the big man I need to know that you're not wearing a wire under that stupid hat. If you're not down then you can leave.'

I exhale deeply with an undercurrent of frustration before stretching out my arms. The bouncer steps forward and mechanically pats me down from top to bottom and back again. Along the way he doesn't say a word. His expression gives nothing away and each prod from his sausage fingers makes my heart jump.

Just when I think he's done, he begins methodically going through my jacket pockets. He unbuttons my top left pocket, taking my black plastic pocket mirror, dental floss and near-empty packet of Orbit chewing gum in his right hand. The bouncer examines the items with contempt before putting them back and, rather strangely, buttoning the pocket back up.

He repeats this routine with the remaining top and bottom pockets on both sides, in turn discovering more packs of Orbit, a small folded pile of Starbucks napkins, A HSBC UK Advance debit card and three ten-dollar bills. Before long he makes a move for my inside pockets, opening out each side of my jacket with one hand while rifling through the contents with the other.

His fat fingers run over a bookmarked copy of Virgil's *The Aeneid* on one side and a copy of Zadie Smith's *Swing Time* on the other with two black A5 writing pads behind it, each one with a grey and black pen clipped to the front. He pulls the tip pad out and begins to flick through the pages.

'What is this shit, poetry? That's so gay.'

The bouncer hands me back the pad while grimacing and I put it back in my pocket.

'You forgot the hat.'

After flashing me a contemptuous glare he takes the straw cowboy hat in his massive right palm and slowly places it on his shiny bald head. He takes a moment to look at me and enjoy his victory before turning around and opening the door. I wait for a verbal invitation to follow but it doesn't come. When he looks back over his left shoulder from just inside the doorstep I follow on cue.

He takes a short step to the right, allowing me to pass on his left before slamming the door shut behind us once he's out of my field of vision.

'On your left.'

I turn in and enter a room on my left. On the far side I see a wiry man with a jarhead haircut in a leopard print robe snorting a line of cocaine off a glass table from left to right through a rolled-up bill. Once the last of the white powder has disappeared, he throws himself back into the sofa, gasping loudly while tilting his head back. He quietly bugs out for a few moments before turning his head to the right and fixing his gaze on me while reaching for a credit card.

'Who the fuck are you?'

'I'm Michael. I have a business proposition for you.'

'A business proposition. How formal.'

'I take it you're Raven Garcia.'

'You take it right. Sit down.' As he says this, he gestures with his right hand rather nonchalantly towards a leather armchair on his right. I walk over and seat myself as Raven prepares another line of cocaine, one which disappears just as quickly as the last and prompts some errant shaking of the head. 'My my, that's some good shit!'

'You want?'

'Nah, I'm good. Had steak and eggs at Denny's for breakfast.'

'Denny's?'

'Yeah.'

'Fuck Denny's!'

'OK.'

'We ain't got no steak and eggs. Up in here we serve ice cream.'

'I see.'

'No, you don't see. I just told you.'

'OK.'

'You said that already.'

The knot in my stomach twists hard in the face of Raven's growing irritability. He's unnaturally vigilant and alert amid the rapid-fire speech and wild hand movements. I'm nervous but at the same time eager to cut to the chase, failing to see how he could poke holes in my generous proposal.

'So, you say you've got a proposition for me. Come on, King Charles. Hit me with something.'

'Treasure Island. I want it.'

'The fuck?'

'Hear me out here. My partner and I will buy out your patch. Today. We've got $60,000 cash which is all yours, plus 10% of our take into perpetuity. Payable weekly. Over the next year you're looking at almost

$750,000, and all you have to do is walk to your mailbox. Your 10% then will be worth more than your 100% now.'

'Is that so?'

'Yes, it is. We're going to shut down your little redneck and turnip truck operation, and in its place will be an exclusive high-end boutique. We run the show, you take a cut. By Christmas we'll be the talk of the town.'

'Why the fuck should I sell to you?'

'I know you're into some bad people for some major dough. The bikers for one. A steady trickle of cash like this and all your problems will go away.'

'$60,000 cash today?'

'Yes.'

'And 10% of your take?'

'That's right.'

'Where's the cash?'

'It's nearby.'

'Alright. We'll have a drink to toast our new partnership. Then we'll get the cash.'

'Thanks, but I don't drink.'

'BUFORD! BRING IN THE HENNY!'

'Honestly, it's alright-.'

'If I'm drinking, you're drinking. Unless you're a cop....'

'No. No, of course not.'

'We're gonna be partners. I need to know that I can trust you.'

'You can trust me.'

Buford comes over with two glasses full of bright orange liquid fire. I take one in my left hand and Raven takes the other.'

'PARTNERS!' Raven shouts this as though it's a battle cry, rising to his feet and raising his glass high in his right hand. I stand up to clink glasses rather sheepishly. He bashes his glass against mine, creating a loud clang as cognac spills out on both sides.

'DOWN THE HATCH!'

He raises his glass above his head and stares at me with an air of expectation. After a few moments I realise this and raise my own glass. Raven begins to slowly move his glass closer to his mouth. I match him move for move before we stop just short of the mark. The game of chicken I never knew I was playing quickly resumes.

I eye Raven for another moment before downing my drink in one while he remains unmoved. The poison swill burns my throat and sends a sharp shudder through my chest. I double over and wheeze loudly while a dagger-sharp throb pierces my temple. This prompts a hearty laugh from Raven, who then downs his own drink in one.

The bitter taste lingers in my mouth as I regain composure. I look straight ahead and steady my gaze, readjusting my poker face as Raven returns his.

'So, we going to get that money or wh-.'

CHAPTER 9

Glass smashes. The room spins. A cream white hue from the plush shag carpet that was beneath my feet fills my view. As everything falls out of focus and powders out into black, a delayed pang hits the back of my head. Sound drains from all directions, filling the blank void with silence.

It's the penultimate Sunday in March and the dials on my watch both hover around the six. The sky's hue imbues neither the damask of night nor the first azure of day, but something unfinished that sits awkwardly between the two. Barely a car lines the roads and in their place is a vacuum of unnerving silence.

I'm all alone once again after a frenetic all-nighter, bereft of the thing I was chasing but too tired to keep running. Flashes of fleeting fun fell through my fingers under the gaudy eighties-tinted disco lights of Popworld and again after hours in the pitch-black thrash metal den of London Stone.

I ended up in London Stone by myself after losing my colleagues in Popworld. We went there for Anne's birthday. Anne from Sales. I've always liked her. I really got into the spirit of the era, with my black vest top in the fashion of Patrick Swayze in *Dirty Dancing* and striped retro headband which didn't come home with me. A pretty blonde girl I was dancing with threw it into the crowd. One of my abiding memories of the night is of a jovial black gentleman in full pimp regalia, complete with cane, who was kind enough to take a photo with me.

At around three in the morning, I was ejected from the club following a genuine misunderstanding. A bouncer who looked like David Haye saw me trip going up the stairs. He took this to mean had I'd had a little bit too much to drink, even though I'd been sipping nothing but Heineken Zero all night long. It didn't help that earlier on Jason was standing right next to me throwing back eyeball shots of tequila and B-52s.

Not quite done for the night, I WhatsApp my colleagues goodbye before going for a wander. My insightful self-reflection, which took me all around the vistas of Bank and Cannon Street, was abruptly halted by the sudden discovery of London Stone. A dark stairwell just inside the front door, leading downstairs to a new unknown.

All around me in the dimly-lit basement I see long hair swinging in the air to Guns & Roses and inflatable guitars. A man emerges from a hidden boor behind a bookshelf and heads for the bar.

I'm not yet ready to face Sunday and figure 'Where better to not face it for a few hours than here?' The pungent aroma of stale beer clings to the atmosphere as the foreground becomes a blurred mass of black denim and sandy blonde hair. Within minutes I have an inflatable guitar in my hand and I'm shaking my non-existent locks to *Smells Like Teen Spirit*.

Once the club closed at half five, I made my way on foot towards Shadwell, thinking of breakfast at the 24-hour McDonald's. I look at my phone and send a series of WhatsApp messages to friends that won't be picked up for hours. The streets are asleep with barely a canned rustle of scant human traffic, the silence filling up with memories of what was and imaginings of what might have been.

Even after everything else, I can't help but keep thinking of the man in the pimp costume.

A cold snap of freezing water sharply scratches my face. I gingerly open my eyes to see the blurred figures of Raven and Buford standing before me. Buford is holding a clear spray bottle in his right hand. Unable to move my arms, I look down to see silver duct tape across my chest mounting me to a chair. My initial confusion gives way to panic and terror while faint recollections of what came before come and go.

I've never seen this room before. A colourless and skeletal shell of bare, exposed timber. No windows, no cool air. A single lightbulb in the centre of a ceiling with a short string next to it half-fills the daunting space with mangy yellow light. I can barely keep my eyes open as Buford and Raven hover ominously in the foreground. The steely gleam reflecting from the silver pistol resting in Raven's waistband hurts my eyes and shoots a shudder of dread into the pit of my stomach.

'Well now, Mr Poet, ha ha. How's that business proposition working out for you?' He snarls with a smug, knowing smile as he speaks. 'Just who do you think you are, motherfucker? You come into my house and disrespect me! Talking about MY BUSINESS!! Telling me about MY SITUATION WITH THE FUCKING VALKYRIES!! Trying to strong-arm me out of MY TERRITORY!!'

My heart rushes and the blood drops from my face. I can think of nothing beyond the present moment.

'How the fuck do you know about The Valkyries? DID THEY SEND YOU?!'

'I don't know anything about any Valkyries. Please.'

'You sure as shit know something. I was flicking through your little scribble book. All this talk of good and evil, scorechasers, demons. What are you, some kind of vigilante? You trying to pull some *Dexter* shit up in here?'

'You're out of your mind.'

'NO, YOU'RE OUT OF YOUR MIND! YOU THINK YOU CAN COME UP IN HERE AND TELL ME WHAT'S WHAT?'

Awkward silence. Is he actually waiting for an answer?

'HUH?'

I suppose he is.

'Look, Raven, I came here with the best of intentions. All I wanted was to do business with you. That's all.'

'Do business with me? All I see you doing is trying to fuck me from behind! Talking about what I owe those biker hicks. How did you hear about that?'

'You just told me.'

'Let's try that again!'

Raven pulls the gun from his waistband and points it right at me. My heart races at the sight of the steel in his hand but quickly settles again upon seeing his tell.

'I see you still want to do business.'

'Excuse me?'

'You still want to do business. Otherwise, you'd have taken the safety off. I know what you're trying to do. You want that money. You need that money. But first you need to see how full of shit I am and convince yourself that you're holding all the cards.'

All the while one thought keeps running through my head:

WHERE THE FUCK IS LOLA?

'You gonna tell me how you heard what you did or am I gonna have to pistol-whip it outta ya?'

Not loaded either.

'Your girls like to talk.'

'I don't pay those bitches to talk.'

'You don't pay them at all.'

'What was I saying about them talking too much?'

'Exactly. That's what I mean. You don't need leaks like that in your organization. I'm fresh off the jumbo jet and I know a little bit about your problems. Imagine what your enemies on those streets know. Sell to me and you'll have one less problem.'

'You talk a good game.'

'No games. Your drug deals with the bikers could really blow up and be big business. Do you want these blabbermouths sniffing around, knowing what you're up to?'

'I hear you.'

'So whaddya say we do business?'

'Sixty grand cash today? For real?'

'Yes. My partner is nearby with the cash.'

'Who's your partner?'

'You don't need to know.'

'Alright.'

'Alright?'

'Yeah. I mean, I don't like not knowing who I'm doing business with. Doesn't mean I'm gonna say no. Oh no. For that the price goes up to $75,000. You give me sixty today and the rest before the weekend.'

He's flexing. He's trying to assert an illusion of control, even with me tied to his chair. He wants to feel like he's in charge, and I'm going to let him.

'You've got yourself a deal.'

A nervous pause while the jury considers their verdict.

'We good?'

'Once I have the sixty grand in my hand, we good.'

That's simple enough.

'OK.'

'You go and get the sixty grand and bring it here. You and Buford.'

'Sure. You might want to untie me first.'

'I'll untie you when I'm fucking ready!'

Flexing again. I'm going to humour him and say nothing.

'Alright.'

The doorbell buzzes unexpectedly, sending a startling rattle through the room which visibly irritates Raven.

'WHAT THE FUCK?' Raven stops shaking and steps towards a silent Buford, eyeballing him momentarily. 'WHAT THE FUCK ARE YOU WAITING FOR?' he shouts while erratically waving his gun in his right hand. 'GO UP THERE AND SEE WHO IT IS!' Buford, sullen and stoic, bows his head down before opening the door and heading up the stairwell.

'FUCK!'

To-do list: Fifteen grand for this psycho we'll hopefully never see again.

Raven stands before me again, his gun back in his waistband. Another awkward silence passes for several minutes, one which we both know from the look on the other's face that there is no need to fill. He pulls a small vial from his trouser pocket with his right hand and prepares a small bump of white powder on the top of his left. After slowly snorting the coke, Raven rapidly throws his head back and mutters something unintelligible while jerking about on the spot.

A goofy smile spreads across Raven's face once he settles, further accentuating the sore redness of his nostrils and the uneven patches of white residue below.

'Fuck yeah.' The last syllable rattles off into a delayed drawl before turning into a loudly maniacal cackle. His lone laughter lock-in abruptly ends after the sound of a cracked, quickfire shot rings out from upstairs. The shot stuns us both, with Raven briskly turning his head over his left shoulder and looking at the door.

'The fuck is that?'

Raven draws the gun from his waistband with his right hand, clearly forgetting that it's not loaded. He lifts his gun up with both hands, the cannon pointing towards the ceiling, before slowly inching towards the door from the left of it. Just before reaching the other end of the room, a slow rumble like a moving bowling ball whirrs from the other side of the door. The rumble ends with an abrupt thud which creates a crack at the bottom of the door. An already wired Raven flinches at the sound.

Raven slowly opens the door from right to left with a hint of paranoid trepidation, no doubt heightened by the copious amounts of nose candy. As the door opens, I see the unconscious body of Buford roll onto its back from left to right until his lifeless eyes are facing the ceiling. Blook slowly flows from a single hole in his chest towards his stomach. A stunned Raven kneels down to look at Buford before being blasted onto his back by three unseen gunshots. His head cracks against the floor while blood flows in two directions from the conjoined bullet holes in his chest.

CHAPTER 10

Shock and terror erode the distance between this moment and the relative normality of what came right before the bloodshed, while at the same time making silent shadows of everything else. A chilling quiet permeates the dank basement as blood pools around the bodies of Buford and Raven. The light from the stairwell cuts through the grisly atmosphere and shines brightest upon a pair of tanned feet in Louboutins perched on a distant step.

'LOLA?'

The beautifully-manicured feet come down the steps, making a loud clacking sound and revealing more of Lola's familiar sight by the second. Her hands are clasped tightly in front of her slender waist as they clutch a shiny black gun.

'LOLA, WHAT THE FUCK?'

'You're welcome.'

'You just killed those two guys!'

'Yeah. Two guys who were gonna kill you.'

'No.'

'What?'

'They weren't going to kill me.'

'What do you mean?'

'We made the deal. I was about to head out with Buford to get the sixty grand.'

'Is that why you're in the basement tied to a chair?'

'It's complicated. Things didn't go so well at first.'

'I can see that.'

'Raven accused me of disrespecting him, trying to strong-arm him with what I know about his little problem with the bikers.'

'What?'

'Yeah. All that coke has made him crazy paranoid. Anyway, what took you so long?'

'Wow! Talk about gratitude!'

'We said fifteen minutes.'

'I was on the phone to the babysitter. She had a question about Jennifer's juice boxes.'

'So, let me get this straight: these two men are dead because of juice boxes?'

'How do you figure? It sounds to me like I would have walked in on them fixing to kill you if I'd been any earlier. Anyway, what happened to closing the deal in fifteen minutes?'

'Like I said, things went bad. He was coked out of his mind.'

'That sounds like Raven. His girls tell me he's got a nose for the stuff like a vacuum.'

'Are you planning to untie me?'

'Yeah. Right.'

Lola trots towards me before stopping behind my chair and beginning to tear away the tape. After about a minute my hands are free. I immediately pull the tape off the front of my shirt and throw it to the floor before slowly rising to my feet. Slightly disoriented from the earlier blow to the head, I turn around and look at Lola.

'Now what?'

'Now what? Now we leave.'

'I don't think so Lola.'

'Are you fucking kidding me?'

'We've got two dead bodies here. We can't just up and leave. No way. We have to figure out how we make this go away so it doesn't come back to us.'

'Do you honestly think that the cops care about a dead pimp and his bodyguard? Unless we're found here holding the smoking gun, we're in the clear.'

'Wrong. The cops will care about a dead pimp and bodyguard, but they won't care about a missing pimp and bodyguard. We have to get rid of the bodies.'

'The cops will just assume that a rival gang did this. Probably those bikers. Raven had a lot of enemies, so the list of people who would want to do this is endless.'

'Wrong. The bullets match your registered gun. Our hairs and fibres are all over the place. We have to fix this.'

'What do you suggest?'

'We need to clean up the basement so that it doesn't become a crime scene and bury the two bodies far from here.'

'I suppose we could drive them out to Red Rock or, better still, Death Valley.'

'Yes, but first we need to take care of this room.'

'We'll need some supplies for this. Hazmat suits, bonesaws, plastic sheeting, heavy duty garbage bags, mops, bleach, shovels....'

I catch Lola off guard with a look of sheer amazement. She is truly formidable.

'What? I studied forensic science.'

'Of course.'

'First, though, we need to get rid of these clothes.'

'What about my cowboy hat?'

'I'll get you a new one.'

'OK.'

'Let's look through Raven's wardrobe for something half-decent.'

'While we're at it we should look for some cash too, to pay for the supplies.'

'We've got plenty of cash in the car.'

'That's our cash which we withdrew this morning. We can't have the serial numbers on those bills being directly traceable from the bank to the bonesaws and bleach. Raven's bills will have been out of the financial system for a while and probably got moved around quite a bit before. The last thing we want is to draw attention to ourselves, so we need to buy things piecemeal. Different items, different stores.'

'There's no wat all that stuff is going to fit in my trunk.'

'Let's take Raven's SUV.'

'So, your idea to avoid drawing attention involves driving around from store to store to store in a dead pimp's SUV.'

'Stay under the speed limit and we'll be fine.'

'You've got it all figured out.'

'You got any better ideas?'

'The cops will have no interest in solving this case. Once they realise Raven's dead, they'll throw a party. Sure, they'll open an investigation. Officially. But they won't want to be seen wasting time and money on a dead pimp and his bouncer. Not when there are so many unsolved missing children's cases in Vegas.'

'We cannot take that chance. These two bodies have got to go.'

'Alright. Alright. If we're going to do this then we need to make sure that the stores are close to one another. We need to get back here fast. Real fast, especially in that car. We also need to do something with Raven's car once we're done dumping the bodies.'

'Long-term parking at McCarran. We wipe it clean first and then we drive it wearing only their clothes. Their clothes, their fibres.'

'We can book him a one-way flight to Bangkok.'

'Yes. He was chopping up coke with his credit card earlier. It's on the table upstairs. We use that to book the flight.'

'OK.'

'By this time tomorrow it'll be as though this never happened.'

We look at one another in agreement. I am impressed and unnerved by Lola's poise in this tense situation.

So formidable.

When the victory comes at too high a price, does the gold smelt in the hands of the victor? Burning their palms with morbid impressions of the scars they left on others.

CHAPTER 11

Bruno Mars blasts from the car stereo and fills the tense silence as Lola and I reflect upon what we've done and what we're about to do. The shock hits me with a delayed fuse reaction, filling my thoughts with memories of Raven and Buford interspliced with images of their lifeless bodies. Soon what was very much living and breathing will sink into an abyss of desert sand, never to be seen again.

Lola, eyes behind Chloe shades, drives with an air of steely authority. Dressed in black from hood to sole in Raven's baggy clothes, we are mirror images of one another. Leather gloves conceal her smooth hands as they glide across the steering wheel. She reaches across with her right hand and mechanically flicks a button to turn the music up.

The car slows and we end up joining a line with a dozen others. In the distance I see a blockade of parked cop cars. Uniformed officers are checking documents, administering breathalyser tests, and waving vehicles through. Lola turns off the music as the car slowly eases to a halt. The vehicles in front slowly move forward. After a moment's hesitation, Lola does the same as a horn aggressively honks in the background.

Cars on either side ominously roll forward in the manner of a funeral procession. I nervously glance at Lola's handbag resting by her feet, thinking about the loaded gun inside it. How many bullets remain and how quickly can Lola floor it? Can I slide the hammer back in good time? These are the kind of thoughts that never even circled my mind yesterday, but the two dead bodies in the basement have somehow skewed my sense of reason.

Lola looks both ways as we inch closer to the front. A fresh-faced male cop signals for the cars in the lane to our left to move into the next lane along. The cars glide further left while Lola stares at the left-hand wing mirror. She flashes a side-eye at the rear-view mirror before glancing again at the left wing and performing an abrupt U-turn into the space which fortuitously opened up beside us.

We go headlong into the tide of incoming cars, swerving past a building cacophony of horns and obscenities. A broad smile breaks out across Lola's face and she relaxes her shoulders. The cop cars slowly fade from the rear-view mirror while we look both ways for a turn. Once the last cop car slips from our vision, we make a turn to the right. We exchange a look of sheer relief upon completing the turn.

By pure chance alone we avoided certain doom. Is that what this life is going to be, a total crap shoot where even the winning dice throws lead to dead bodies in the desert? One week ago, I was contemplating whether or not to have that fifth go-round on the *Jurassic Park* ride at Universal LA. Today I'm burying bodies with my beautiful new wife.

Life is full. Full or surprises.

Darkness falls and settles into the perfect mix of noir and night ocean blue. The watercolour hue of the sky illuminates the natural beauty of the Santa Cruz forestry on all sides. Pro drives along the curling coastal roads while Andre sits in the back of our rented black Dodge Charger and I flit in and out of sleep on the passenger side. The road is largely deserted, eliciting a tranquillity at odds with the buzz of our afternoon at Pier 39 back in San Francisco.

A strange feeling washes over me, a nice sense of contentment but at the same time anticipation ahead of our arrival in Monterey. The open packet of Twizzlers in between the seats blurs out of my view while the full weight of the day bears down on my eyelids. I rest my right check against the window while slouching in my seat.

I close my eyes and strange shapes begin to form in the foreground. The nondescript visions fly right at me, shifting from a foetal pink to orange to grey and then to black as they inch ever closer. Before long, the colours collapse into one another and quickly separate, like pixels fading to reveal a hitherto blurred image in all of its clear splendour.

I take in the curvature of the winding road, watching it disappear from the window one square at a time, only to be replaced by an identical one each time. A snap thrust of wind marks the spot every few seconds, like a hand on a clock pacing down towards something amazing.

A fuzzy shadow reminiscent of a Rorschach Test forms ahead of me and turns a corner. It crawls forward with eery deliberation, coming into focus as it edges closer to our Charger. The scrawled and scratchy patches of black connect, and a mirror image of our car materialises. It's coming right at us. No time to swerve.

'LOOK OUT!'

Lola flashes me a startled look of concern as I wake up in a wet chill.

'You OK, baby?'

'Yeah, yeah. I'm fine.'

'We're almost there. Don't worry.'

'Yep. Almost there.'

The nose of a cop car eases into the rear-view. I think nothing of it until suddenly the lights flash and the sirens begin to wail. Lola slows down almost on cue when the cop car glides to our left, mildly gritting her teeth while dropping speed. The patrol car is now right next to us. Knowing looks are exchanged between Lola and the cop before we slow to a smooth stop, prompting the lights and sirens to peter out.

I see the cop car stop behind us and the officer leave the car to approach on our left. Once again, I look at Lola's handbag, thinking about her gun. Lola checks herself in the mirror before winding down the window ahead of the incoming cop's arrival.

'License and registration.'

The cop is a pretty Seneca woman with mahogany skin and short black hair, clad in a dark blue pantsuit with a gold shield hanging from her neck. Her saucer-like brown eyes give nothing away and no expression escapes from her generous lips.

Lola nervously passes the documents to the cop with her right hand. The cop looks at them long and hard before shooting Lola an ambiguous glance. She cans the documents again before handing them back.

'Alexa Linda Velez. This clearly isn't your car.'

'No Officer.'

'It's Sergeant. If this were your car, you'd know that.'

What?

'I'm going to need you to step out of the vehicle. Both of you.'

'Sure thing, Officer.'

'It's Sergeant. Sergeant Diana Redclay, Alexa.'

'OK.'

We slowly leave the vehicle while Redclay looks on, being sure not to do anything that would alarm her further.

'Hands on the vehicle where I can see them.'

No sooner said than done.

'Hoods down. Shades off.'

Again.

'Don't move.'

Redclay pats Lola down from head to toe before rifling meticulously through her pockets. She frowns after finding nothing.

'Every time I see this car, I see a different one of Raven's whores behind the wheel. They always have a brown envelope and two keys of blow for me.'

Just like that, my heart drops. We've found the one cop who has a vested interest in Raven being alive. Or rather she found us. No coincidence.

'Pass me the keys.'

Lola opens the door and pulls the keys from the ignition before slowly handing them to Redclay. She takes the keys and walks around to the boot of the SUV, briefly leaving my field of vision. The trunk pops open and all I can hear are rustling and rummaging sounds. I stare again at Lola's handbag, thinking of ways to covertly grab her gun.

This is it. The end of a road we barely travelled down. We didn't want this, but there's no other way. I really wish there was.

'Hah.'

Lola's sigh is a welcome but sadly brief break from my train of deathly thought. I look right at her and then down at the handbag inside the car, trying to convey my intentions. All I can elicit is a passing look of sullen confusion from my beloved. I momentarily look back at the water bottles from Raven's kitchen.

I manage to slowly and quietly pull back the door handle with my right hand. The door slides outwards without making a sound before I lean my upper body inside and over the passenger seat. My fingers have barely grazed the purse by the time I've found the gun and taken it in my right palm. Upon looking up I see Lola through the window. Her eyes are full of regret and her head is slowly shaking. I pause momentarily to take in her misgivings before being interrupted by an ominous click.

'Hold it right there!'

No.

'That's quite a shop you've done. Plastic sheeting, saws, bleach. Home improvement project?'

'Something like that.'

'Or is Raven burying bodies again?'

I let out a nervous laugh.

'You probably noticed that I didn't care enough to pat you down. I had you down as the loser simp boyfriend who's just now finding out that his out of his league girlfriend doesn't really work at Target. I still do, by the way.'

Wow.

'But check out the big balls on you! You were gonna pop a cop right here in broad daylight. Now you've got me interested. Who are you?'

'I'm The Money Man.'

'What the fuck?'

'I'm just an accountant.'

'An accountant? You think you're fucking funny?'

Yes.

'Who are you and what the fuck are you doing in Raven's car with no cash and no snow for me?'

Time to bullshit.

'We're associates of Raven. Just holding the fort while he does his business out of town. You would know that if you were that close.'

Silence. I've rattled her.

'He didn't tell you about his business out of town?'

'Bullshit.'

That's not good.

'Looks like he ghosted you.'

The trunk slams shut. She's angry.

'What do you know about Raven?'

'Like I said, we're business associates.'

'He never mentioned an associate from England.'

'Really? The guy who ghosted you never mentioned me?'

'Alright, smart man. You tell your associate I'll be back this day next week. He owes me for two weeks now, plus the vig for this week. Until then, this car is going into impound. The Valkyries would pay me double what Raven owes me to find something in the trunk's false bottom that could take him off the streets for a few years.'

So much for staying under the speed limit.

'Wait!' interjects Lola with a real vigour. 'We have money. Whatever Raven owes you, we'll take care of it.'

'What about my two keys?'

'Sorry Diana. I can't help you there. But we have $60,000 in cash. It's in my car. Follow us back to Raven's house and we can get it.'

My Lola.

'I know where it is. You follow me.'

I hear a sudden click, identical to the first one, followed by a clipping sound which I hope is her holster being fastened. Dainty fingers tickle my ribs and hips as Diana frisks me. While her hands are gliding up and down my body, I look at Lola again through the window and we each show a smile which tells the other that everything's going to be alright.

Why do we lie to one another?

CHAPTER 12

We trail Redclay's cop car for what seems like an eternity, my heart racing each and every time her taillights flash. So far, we've made three turns which Lola didn't recognise. Where are we going? Does Redclay not believe us about the money? Is she leading us into a trap? After she caught me reaching for Lola's gun, Redclay has every reason to want to kill us before we kill her. She could have done it during the stop and search. But she didn't.

It's not too late for us to cut our losses. We just need to get through this. Once the bodies are buried and Redclay's been paid off, we can skip town. Start over in London. I can contract, Lola can dance at The Nag's Head in Whitechapel, and we can work towards eventually being real estate investors. Exactly like we said, except back home.

A new beginning looms. Not the one we had planned, but a fresh start nonetheless. A wife, a stepdaughter and a path which is mine and mine alone. The holiday breathed new life into me, fitting as our last stop was the city of second chances. I have to make good on what I've learned out here. One last speed bump to get over and then the slate is wiped clean.

Suddenly a blacked-out Hummer comes into the rear-view. Almost ghost-like was its abrupt left-hand turn. We slow down and eventually halt upon seeing

Redclay's lights flash, yet the Hummer picks up speed and only stops at the last moment. By then it is less than half a car's distance behind us, halogens beaming at full blast.

Redclay's lights stop flashing and her car is rooted to the spot. The Hummer remains still, and the loitering halogens don't blink an inch. Only three bullets sit in the chamber of Lola's gun. We have no idea how many goons are in the Hummer. There's not enough space for us to make a half-decent turn and build up enough initial speed to lose them both. We're trapped.

The taillights go out. All we can do is wait. A nervous pause while the executioner stops to take a breath. The kind of reprieve which is just as cruel as what follows, for all it does is give the condemned man a few moments longer to scan the gallows. That prolonged gaze at the instrument of his demise just before the inevitable occurs is truly brutal, for they rob the dead man walking of any chance to enjoy some happy last thoughts.

We're on the move again. The Hummer follows less closely for about a minute and then slinks off into a sharp turn to the right. Who was that, and what did they want? The messes are piling up. Just as we veer towards the light at the end of the tunnel, a much darker crevice looms.

Redclay's next turn provides relief, for she steers us onto the more familiar home stretch towards the scene of our crimes. I can just about see Lola's car in the distance. Lola and I mark the comfortable silence by sharing a warm, relaxed glance. For the first time in my life, I've found love.

While Redclay steers left into Raven's driveway, Lola prepares to park in front of her own car. We pull in and watch as Redclay parks up and sits in the stationary squad car. She's loitering, intimidating, and we're at least trying to do the same right back.

We watch and wait. And wait. And wait. I reach for Lola's gun and carefully tuck it into my pocket. Three in the chamber. It only takes one.

'What the fuck is she waiting for?'

Lola, visibly restless and agitated, flashes our lights as an invitation to Redclay. She doesn't bite. I gently roll the hammer back with the ball of my right thumb. We flash twice more before sitting in darkness. Redclay finally steps out of the car and slowly approaches. I notice a space in her holster as she draws closer. My grip on the gun tightens at the same time that Lola winds her window down slightly. Her left hand stretches out, gripping the car keys, and almost on cue two short chirps sound as the trunk of Lola's car pops open ahead of us.

Redclay changes direction and heads towards Lola's car. She opens the boot right up and then unzips the black gym bag. Her right hand shuffles over the piles of bills for several seconds. Seemingly satisfied, she zips up the bag, takes it out in her right hand and closes the trunk with her left. All business, Sergeant Redclay turns around and pulls in next to Lola.

'Tell me what the fuck is going on.'

Huh?

'There's $60,000 in the bag. Raven only owes me $3,000, plus my two keys of blow. But you already know that, being such close business associates of his.'

This is not good.

'I called Raven's cell when I was over there in his driveway. Heard it ring through the window.'

Shit.

'His cell? Which one?' I chime.

'Shut the fuck up!'

I check with my fingers to see if the safety is off.

'You lied to me, and I'm out two keys. Whaddya say we go in there and get 'em?'

'We can get you another $15,000, cash, before the weekend.'

'You're not buying me off. I don't care about Raven or what's happened to him. I've got ten more scumbags just like him in rotation. I celebrate with blow and a few whores whenever one of these bangers gets popped.'

The irony.

'This can go down in one of two ways.'

This trigger makes I three.

'We can go in there now, all three of us, and I can collect my two keys from Raven. Alternatively, we could say no more about Raven and you two can assume his debt to me.'

She knows, but she can't prove anything.

'You want us to pay you three grand a week?' Lola is incredulous.

'Don't forget my two keys.'

'We don't run drugs. We run girls.'

'That's too bad. I guess I'll just have to take my two keys' worth in free entertainment.'

'What the fuck would we be paying you for?'

'To watch your ass.'

'Our ass?'

'Yeah. Your ass.'

This should be good.

'I'll be your eyes and ears in Vegas P.D. Vice. My detectives, my officers, your hired guns. We're the ones who make the heat go away and turn it up where you want it turned up.'

The bullshit is strong with this one.

'Your three grand a week will ensure that any investigation into your operation dies on the file clerk's desk. We'll keep an eye out for competitors looking to poach on your territory and get them out of your way. You give us a name, say the word, and it's done. I'm talking all guns blazing, shock and awe, Custer's last stand.'

Can we trust her?

'How do we know we can trust you?'

'You don't.'

And there it is.

'But for three grand a week, you'll get three grand's worth of peace of mind. For the right multiplier, I'll give you fucking Nirvana!'

She's good.

'How about you fucking earn it?'

My Lola.

'Excuse me?'

'You heard me!'

The horns lock and first blood is about to fall.

'We'll give you two grand a week against five points from our take. Right out of the gate you'll be making more than triple your two-grand guarantee.'

'Bullshit.'

'I bullshit you not, but first you've got to audition.'

Redclay's face is a picture of Sphinx-like granite.

'I'll name a patch on the strip. You knock it down by this time next week and you've got a deal.'

'Why should I give you a free sample?'

'We're looking at high seven figures for the first year alone. This is a chance for you to get in on the ground floor.'

I watch as Redclay's iron gaze softens slightly.

'You don't have to give us a free sample. But if you don't, well, a recording of your earlier offer will end up somewhere inconvenient.'

Hook. Line.

'Tell me the patch and I'll knock it down by the end of next week.'

Sinker.

'I'll tell you when I'm ready.'

'Alright, partner.'

'Alright, junior partner.'

I love this woman.

'Whaddya say we go check on the merchandise? I wanna see my five points in the flesh.'

'Tomorrow.'

'You got something better to do right now?'

Apart from dismembering and disposing of two dead bodies, no.

'Follow us.'

Dirty Diana kneels down to tie her right shoelace. Before getting back up, she wipes her right-hand palm against her jacket before wiping it against the bottom of the car.

'Let's roll.'

CHAPTER 13

The atmosphere is like that of a more serene sorority house. Women of various shades fill the room in a variety of mini factions. Some play cards, some play bones. Others eat pizza and drink beer, others smoke pot. There's a little twerking, a little popping and *WAP* is blasting out in the background. An egregious action movie which nobody appears to be watching plays on the plasma screen TV.

'Take a good look at your new gravy train.' Redclay seems to have forgotten that she is our junior partner. Better remind her and fast. 'Honey, get over here.' While Redclay says this she snaps the fingers on her raised right hand several times in rapid succession. At her command, a beautiful Nubian Amazon approaches. She sports a big head of curly natural hair and her short black dress highlights her voluptuous curves.

'Meet Honey, my best earner.' Honey stands before Redclay, defiantly staring a hole through her with eyes like blades. I see an undeniable fire in her aura which is impossible to ignore. 'Time to pony up, doll.' Redclay holds out an open right palm and flicks Honey a look loaded with expectation. A stubborn Honey waits and then reaches between her amble breasts with her right thumb and index finger.

Honey reveals a roll of hundred-dollar bills in a rubber band. She contemptuously slaps the cash into Redclay's hand. Before Redclay can close her palm, I snatch the roll of green from her. She freezes on the spot, stunned, incredulous. I look right back at her while making a show of ripping the rubber band away. Without even thinking about it, I pass half each to Honey and Lola before placing a lone dollar from my pocket in Redclay's hand.

'Let's get something straight, cop. You're a junior partner, not the boss. Don't you ever talk to our employees like that again. Just don't.'

Sergeant Redclay is genuinely taken aback. Honey quickly and quietly retreats.

'From now on these girls will not be treated like circus animals!' Everyone in the room stops what they're doing and looks over when I bellow this. 'These girls work hard for the money, so it's only right that they share in the spoils. Fifty percent commission, payable monthly. No excuses. No exceptions.'

Smiles break out across the room, and I can see hope forming in the eyes of the girls. Hope which I can tell hasn't seen the light of day for years. The plan was to dump the bodies before cutting and running. But not now. As I scan the room from left to right, I see sixteen young women becoming empowered. A match has been struck under their hearts. This fire must burn, and burn hard.

'Your days of answering to Thrift Shop Scarface are over. Nobody owns you. If you don't want to work for us, you don't have to. If you do want to work for us, you will be well taken care of. Please excuse our junior partner here. She clearly forgot her manners when getting ready for work this morning.'

They cling to every last syllable.

'As of today, our business at Treasure Island will begin a two-month period of hiatus.' Lola shoots me a quizzical look, acknowledging that this is not what we discussed before. 'You can consider this a vacation. Go be with your families, recharge your batteries and be ready to return to work on January 1st. Those of you who do return will become founder members of Top Drawer Entertainment.'

Everyone is fired up. I can really feel the energy in the room.

'We are going to offer premium escort services, the likes of which Las Vegas has never seen before. You're going to be targeting high rollers who can afford to pay you $1,000 an hour in minimum blocks of two hours, and you will be a bargain at that price. Your commission will be 50%, provided that you charge four hours a day, four days a week. Anything less than that and your cut will fall to 25%. It's up to you, but those extra couple of hours make the difference between making $3,500 commission for the week and making $8,000. The difference between buying the Rolls Royce and buying the dealership.'

A rose of hyperbole blooming from the soil of sincerity.

'Sixteen chargeable hours a week. That will be your mission for 45 weeks a year. You're all independent contractors. You work for yourselves. Each one of you will be paid a weekly guarantee of $1,000. Effective immediately.

Smiles and quiet yelps of delight break out among the girls. A slither of silent scepticism, fully understandable, escapes from the restrained cheers.

'Your lives are about to change. Say goodbye to this house. Start looking for your own apartments. We'll take care of the security deposits and first three months of rent. Hell, we'll even put a cherry on top for new furniture. If any of you have substance problems or outstanding legal issues, talk to Lola and I confidentially. We will take care of you, financially and otherwise.'

Redclay scoffs and shakes her head.

All of those perks will be made available to any of you who decide to stay and work for us. Should you decide not to stay on, we will write you a cheque for $150,000. Any and all remainers will receive private medical insurance, dental cover and a 10% non-contributory pension plan. You'll also receive a cheque for $25,000, a golden hello which I encourage you to spend on new designer clothes before January.'

Lola looks up at me, her eyes full of warmth, and mouths 'I'm so proud of you.' Honey, now with the rest of the girls, confidently raises her right hand. I signal back to her with my right index finger and a smile.

'Who are you?'

Another lunch hour breaking up another dull day at the office. Just me and a good book. William Blake. My eyes can breathe again in the absence of pivot tables and seemingly endless formulae. I spent the hour before lunch reconciling the miscellaneous staff loans account. In other words, calculating how much money the slimeballs in Global Mobility Sales owe the company in repayments for loans to clear their cocaine debts. Most of these loans are deducted monthly from payroll. Until they're not. Others haven't seen a single repayment, and likely never will.

The silence provides welcome respite from the constant peacocking of the alpha minus males on the Global Mobility Sales team. To me they're an alien species. I'm sure I am to them as well. Their patch of the office is a bombastic alcove of bravado, gangsta rap, unjustifiable entitlement and insecure small dick energy.

On any given day you can look over there and see toxic masculinity which is beyond any form of parody or satire. Billy Robson and Darren Ryan, in between coke races at their desks, comparing pictures on their phones of the women they've slept with. Like two kids showing one another their football stickers. How pathetic.

Nataraj Maholtra boasting of his day-long whistlestop sex tours of the West Midlands. Imran Malik rearranging the tub of protein powder and Spearmint Rhino VIP entry card on his desk, hoping that someone walking past will comment. David Danan shoving his empty tins of gin and tonic into his desk drawers alongside unread paperwork while cracking crude jokes. The one he told about the Jewish women in Toronto storing diamonds in intimate crevices was a particular lowlight.

Many days I have gone out to lunch and considered not returning to the part-frat house, part-sewing circle hellhole of an office. I really miss Dev, a fellow John Grisham, theatre and classical music enthusiast. Raj, the chauvinistic pillock who told a female finance apprentice 'Accountancy is for men' is someone I have nothing in common with. So many times, I have fantasized about tearing that wig from his head.

I enjoy Blake's words while trying to not look at the watch on my left hand. When I do, I hope in futility that the hands haven't moved. I love the solitude, the absence of obnoxious noise. It's as though the silence is mine and mine alone.

The words on the page tinkle the ivories of my mind. For these few moments I spend scanning them, it's as if I've turned out a light on a reality in which I'm an outcast and a loser.

A POISON TREE

I was angry with my friend:
I told my wrath, my wrath did end.
I was angry with my foe.
I told it not, my wrath did grow.

And I watered it in fears.
Night & morning with my tears:

And I sunned it with smiles.
And with soft deceitful wiles.

And it grew both day and night.
Till it bore an apple bright.
And my foe beheld it shine.
And he knew that it was mine.

And into my garden stole.
When the night had veild the pole;
In the morning glad I see;
My foe outstretched beneath the tree.

The drive back to Raven's house became an increasingly nervous one. After leaving the house of his hookers, we drove one way and Redclay drove the other. Several minutes later we found Dirty Diana back in our rear-view. But why? She was pretty steamed after I reprimanded her in front of the girls, but she now has $60,000 which she didn't have this morning.

Redclay flashes her lights, trying to show us who's boss. Lola doesn't sell it, maintaining a normal speed in response. We're just a few minutes away from Raven's house and we need to lose Redclay. We can't afford to be caught out here. Something has to give.

I look up ahead to see the green light blinking. Lola and I return a knowing look before returning our eyes to the foreground. The light turns red and Lola floors it straight through. Behind us we see Redclay getting caught between two cars crossing in opposite directions. A male driver wearing a red baseball cap emerges from one of the cars and begins to berate Redclay as we pull away.

My wife flashes me a reassuring smile which breathes a sense of relief into me. In this moment she takes my heart and saddles it in her hands, saddling it in a way that nobody ever has.

'I'm really proud of you. I know you weren't on board at first with all my suggested bells and whistles, given that we're already planning to pay the girls so much money. This really means a lot to me, as someone who has done this for years with none of that security.'

Taken aback, I look at Lola with a coy smile.'

'I love you, Michael.'

'I love you too.'

'I'm just hoping that your seed money idea works. How much did you say, $3 million.'

'Yes. And it will work because I will make it work.'

Lola looks up at me, admiring my confidence.

'For once, my ability to remember useless information will help.'

My wife responds with a quiet laugh.

'I log on as Velma to set up the transfers. Then I log on as Raj to approve them. The money will go to a virtual account in the name of Raj's Indian outsourcing company, RP Group. From there it will go off the grid, being transferred again and again. Eventually it will land in the Cayman Islands and the account of Majestic Ventures, an investment angel who will put up the money for Top Drawer Entertainment in return for an 85% stake.'

Lola presses a button on the car stereo and *Uptown Funk* begins to play.

'I love it' she says. 'We kick 85% of the dividend back to the Caymans. A few transfers and a few trades later, allowing for 10% shrinkage, the cash comes back to the States. Clean, untaxed, untraceable. Nobody will ever know that we own Majestic or find the true source of the seed money.'

We turn left into Raven's driveway. Again. We look all around us and there's no sign of Redclay. All clear.

'Hah.'

Behind that front door are our crimes. Two lives that are no more. In just a few hours they'll be packed neatly into several bin bags and buried in the desert, never to be spoken of again. But does it end there? Will the horrific memory of their cold and lifeless faces tear through the shrink wrap of silent denial? Are the shadows of our momentary misdeeds going to stalk our sleep for years to come? Can we expect reprisals, and are these two dead bodies just the deposit portion of a much greater price to be paid for this life?

Doing nothing will leave Pandora's Box wide open, while the sound of it slamming shut could awaken all kinds of monsters and demons.

CHAPTER 14

Is this how it ends for the bad guys? After violent lives of dirty money and looming threats from all sides, danger which doesn't keep office hours and is just as pernicious in its absence as it is in its presence. A dark world in which every kernel of success is picked from an ominous step on the stairwell to a grisly inevitable. And is this the inevitable? A life that encompassed all the terror and fleeting triumph of a criminal existence, now dismembered, and packed into six black bin bags. No pomp. No fanfare. No mourners.

Lola and I survey the damage. A dozen tightly coiled packages of what used to be bravado, bombast, and pumped-up machismo, now sitting inanimate in the middle of the living room. The Nevada Desert will be the final destination for Raven and Buford. No word of warning, no final farewell and nothing to mark the spot.

The dismembering, wrapping, bagging, and cleaning has built up quite a sweat. A thick, rancid layer of which makes the inside of my hazmat suit cling hard to my body. I head to Raven's kitchen, parched, to grab two bottles of water from the fridge.

I peel back the head of my hazmat suit and as soon as I open the fridge door the cold air hits me hard. For a moment I close my eyes and let the cutting chill engulf me. A most welcome reprieve from the unrelenting sting of enclosed sweat, binding to my face like a viscous second skin.

My need for cool relief now satiated, I pull out the two clear bottles of water and lay them on the kitchen work surface. After slamming the fridge door, shut, I lay my palms on the worktop and close my eyes. I take a deep breath before scanning the water bottles. The passing breeze of fleeting peace washes over me and holds me in its gentle grasp, until an image of something that wasn't on the worktop before suddenly materialises in the corner of my left eye.

An empty beer bottle.

'Shit.'

Someone else was here since we were last here.

'SHIT! SHIT! SHIT! SHIT!'

'What is it?'

I didn't even notice Lola entering the kitchen.

'That beer bottle wasn't here before we left. Someone else was in here.'

'Fuck.'

'Whoever it was, they didn't move the bodies an inch. But we don't know what they saw and who they told.'

'You know something? It could be those bikers Raven had beef with.'

'That would explain why this place isn't a crime scene right now.'

'But what if it wasn't them?'

'Then burying bodies is kind of a moot point. But it needs to be done, so that whoever it was finds nothing when and if they come back.'

We make our way back into the living room and stand by the bags. A Humvee pulls up outside, its high beams slightly piercing the drawn blind. The shadows tease us with a thousand promises of doom. The driver walks around the back of the vehicle before heading for the front door. I grab Lola's gun and make a run for the door, hoping to get there before the shadow does.

After racing to the left of the lock with the gun in my right hand, I slide the chain across with my left to lock the door from the inside. The sound of the chain sliding is drowned out by the noise of a key turning the lock. I jump back towards the wall as the door opens ajar, making a clean as the chain nears its breaking point.

'Fuck me!'

He's frustrated. Who is he and why does he have a key to Raven's house.

'Yo Raven!'

He sticks his head in the door as far as he can. I quietly slide back the hammer, being careful not to make a sound. He lurks menacingly and I point the trigger forward. It would be an awkward shot with little chance of success, save for a lucky ricochet off the wall. At the very least he would recoil at the apparent warning shot and give me time to regroup. As much as I'd like to avoid another dead body, I'm going to do whatever I can to survive this.

The door slams back shut, and the key makes an awful scratching sound on its way out.

'Shit.'

I hear from outside the sounding of phone buttons. He's calling Raven's phone, which is as the bottom of a bin bag between severed limbs. Switched off. He obviously doesn't know that Raven is dead. Was it him who was earlier? Maybe he was here but didn't go to the basement. He had no reason to.

The phone rings momentarily and then goes to voicemail. This aggravates him even further.

'Yo Raven, it's me. Where the fuck are you? Did you get high again? You better get your shit together before tomorrow morning. We can't fuck this up.'

He angrily hangs up.

'Fucker.'

Still in an obvious huff, he retreats to his Humvee. The sound of his engine starting and the vehicle reversing out of the driveway brings me a huge sense of relief. Once I'm confident he is gone, I dart back towards Lola and the black bags in the living room.

'What the fuck was that?' I ask Lola.

'That was Nile. He's Raven's D.L. lover.'

'What?'

'Yep. His secret trap queen. I'm sure I told you before that Raven is gay.'

'I must have forgotten.'

'Raven treats Nile like an errand boy when there are other people around. But we all know what's up. The girls don't care. I don't care. Raven is one of those.'

'One of those what?'

'Self-hating gays.'

'Huh?'

'He sees his homosexuality as a weakness. A perversion. He doesn't want anyone else to know.'

'He sounds troubled.'

'You have to understand. He's a single-minded street guy. To him a gay man has no street credibility. He figures that if he hates what he is so much, then what will everyone else think? People he has to do business with.'

'Why are we still talking about him in the present tense?'

Lola is taken aback by my slight callousness, ironic given that she's the one who killed Raven and got this party started. In many ways her response is assuring. Lola is not a cold-blooded killer devoid of empathy. She's a protector.

'Can you think of anyone else who may have a key to this place?'

'No. Not one.'

'If it was Nile who was here earlier then we're home and dry.'

'Too many ifs.'

Don't sell it.

'He didn't go down to the basement. Saw nothing, knows nothing.'

'Right.'

'Don't look so worried.'

'But what if it wasn't him? What if it was someone else who was here, and they saw the bodies?'

'Now that's too many ifs.'

Lola looks back at me, slightly annoyed.

'Well, these bags aren't going to take themselves to the car.'

We grab two bags each and make our way towards the front door. I put my bags down on the floor and open back the door for Lola to walk through. Once Lola has cleared, I hold the door open with the inside of my right foot and picky my bags back up. Lola places her bags on the ground just behind the car and proceeds to open the trunk. She places her bags inside, followed by mine.

After repeating this ritual twice, we strip off the hazmat suits and throw them in the trunk before slamming it shut. We pull out of the driveway and enjoy a silent high five. The bug spray will disguise the smell of bleach for the most part, assuming that anybody enters the house within the next 48 hours.

Lola turns on the car stereo to *Seven Nation Army* as we roll out washed in a sense of macabre triumph. The girls Raven mistreated would thank us profusely. As for Buford, I guess he just hitched himself to the wrong wagon.

The line has been crossed, and there's no going back. It's a faint line now, barely distinguishable from the asphalt it's painted on, and I wouldn't want to go back if I could.

CHAPTER 15

The drive to Red Rock Canyon proceeds in what feels like slow-motion. Our gorily dismembered cargo weighs heavier on our minds than it does the fuel consumption. I can think of nothing beyond this drive, no tomorrow, not even an immediate aftermath. If we get this wrong, it's all over. If we get this right, then what? Weeks, months and years questioning each day unmarked by our arrest. Are we free because nobody knows? Or because an enemy, or even an ally, is keeping our dark fate in their pocket for another day?

That beer bottle has set my teeth on edge. I want to think it was Nile who left it. Who else could have, and why would they have been there?

We've stopped off at a gas station to load up on water. The evening is hot and unforgiving as a beautiful twilight annexes the last of the daylight. I keep looking nervously out of the window at the SUV. Other cars pass it in both directions, their drivers blissfully unaware of how their white picket fence lives so briefly intersected with the dark side.

I walk around to the next aisle to look for a Three Musketeers bar among the mass of candy. My back is turned towards the entrance when suddenly the bell rings to indicate someone entering the store.

'Hey Lexi. Nice wheels. When did you get the new car?'

Shit.

'Shit.'

This just became too risky. I briskly walk towards Lola and her blonde friend as their jovial chatter continues.

'We have to go. Now.'

Lola looks at me, sensing the terse urgency of my energy.

'Michael, this is my friend Amy. She works at the Treasure Island Starbucks. Amy, this is -.'

'Her husband. Hi. We really have to go.'

I make for the door and let myself out, not looking back at all along the way. The bell has barely stopped ringing by the time I've reached the SUV and turned back to face the store. It rings again as Lola exits, hastening to catch up.

'What was that?' asks a puzzled Lola, arms outstretched. I stay Silent while she quickens her pace towards the car. She finally stops before me with a look of confusion.

'We can't do this Lola. Not like this.'

'What are you talking about?'

'Your friend, Amy. She knows your real name. She can tie us to this car. If anyone asks her, it's pretty obvious where we're going. From here, what are the choices? We're either on our way to Red Rock or we've just left there.'

'It's alright. Amy's on her way home. She lives on the reservation by Red Rock with her husband. He's a tour guide at the canyon.'

'We cannot go on as planned. No way. We just can't.'

'Nobody knows anything. There's no way anybody will make any kind of connection. Amy has no idea where exactly we're going. Nobody has a reason to question her.'

I take a deep breath and close my eyes.

'Besides, you said that nobody with a badge cares about investigating a missing pimp.'

'No. No they don't. But if a whopper of a piece falls into their lap, they will follow up. Amy knows your real name, and she saw us in Raven's car in this general area. We can't give the cops anything to look for out there. This little hiccup has increased our chances of having a conversation with the cops. They cannot find anything beneath the sand.'

'What do you suggest?'

'Not here. Let's talk in the car.'

'OK.'

We get into the SUV and lock the doors. I take a moment to adjust my position so that my back is comfortable.

'We're going to go back to the house and melting the body parts. On the way back we make a few stops and we get the things we need. Obviously, we're going to need sulphuric acid and a bug plastic tub.'

'It's going to take two whole days for the remains to dissolve completely.'

'I'll take care of it. You can drop me off and then go home to Jennifer. I'll call you when it's done.'

'What about this car? We were supposed to leave it at the airport.'

'Fuck it. We can't afford to drive around in this thing much longer. Anyone who cares to look can assume that Raven and Buford took and Uber to the airport.'

'Right.'

'We'll need burner phones for the business. Raven has a whole bunch at the house. Before you go home, we'll clean out the lot.'

'Anyone who's looking for Raven will be blowing up these phones. If we have them, we can stay one step ahead.'

'Exactly.'

'We've got this.'

'We've got this.'

Lola and I share a comfortable silence, one completely at odds with what awaits us, over a smile of mutual assurance. Amidst the carnage, chaos, terror and danger, the dismembered body parts and fallen bullets, we've found love. True love.'

As Lola turns away and twists the key in the ignition, I feel a stolen sense of peace breeze through me. It eases my body while gently taunting me with a faint whisper of something pernicious. Are we heading for the finishing line or are we about to start another race on roads paved with hellfire?

Another day, another boring presentation. Today's is all about brand values. More like bland values. Universal Bloc Manager (whatever the fuck that means) Robert Dawson is running the show today, talking us through a new set on company initiatives that sound like they were lifted from David's Brent dustbin. I'm biting my tongue to both stay awake and keep from laughing out loud. Just before this meeting Andre sent me a hilarious joke about a less-than-intelligent person I once knew.

'If you want to be successful in business, you must have a compelling front end!'

That same stupid joke. It won't be long before he tells the story about the cleaner at NASA.'

'Ha ha ha.'

Every fool laughs at their own jokes. Sadly, nobody else does.

'Now, our first brand value is Kind.'

Bullshit.

'What is Kind?'

Kind is not depleting our already questionable will to live.

'In the context of our business, Kind is…..'

The words collapse into one another until they become nothing but one long nondescript noise. My eyes and my thoughts cling to floating debris of mindless rubbish, desperately trying not to drown in sleep. This goes on for another fifteen or twenty soul-crushing minutes. I look around at the other faces in the room, trying to work out if anyone else feels the same way as me.'

'I'm going to tell you a story now, about the cleaner at NASA.'

The cleaner at NASA helped to put a man on the moon. By killing Raven and Buford, Lola very marginally reduced the world's violent criminality. This provides little to no solace when you're the one pulling their remains out of bin bags.

Back in the basement. The last time I was here Lola and I were preparing for Operation: Red Rock. If I never see this house again it will be far too soon. The tub of acid sits in the middle of the room, hissing steam rising towards the ceiling with a quiet tease of salvation beneath the menace. I sit cross-legged on the floor, slowly and mechanically dropping the severed body parts into the acid one by one. My bare fingers tremble every time I reach across with my right hand and I can never establish a steady grip.

I pick up a tanned arm, bereft of the wrist at one end and the elbow at the other. The cuts on both sides are ridiculously clean and precise. My right arm is trembling more so than before and my panicked breaths can only half escape my lungs. Each puff weighs heavier than the last, the sharp air that doesn't leave being piled upon by that which was meant to replace it. The heavy air makes a jagged lead of my stomach's pit to the point where it hurts turn my torso.

My right arm, still shaking, hovers above the vat of burning acid while clutching the severed arm. It slips from my fingers too soon and the sudden, violent splash causes me to instinctively recoil. I throw my whole body back before landing on my front with my hands in front of my chest. The acid somehow avoids me, but when I look ahead, I see a clear spittle on an exposed floorboard. It bubbles rapidly with a slow hiss.

I see something ominous in the spittle of acid, something which I try to ignore. After a few moments of lying rooted to the spot with my eyes closed, I rise to my feet. Behind me I see the two bin bags containing what's left of Raven and Buford to the right of the acid-filled tub. In a move I should have made several minutes ago, I pick up the two bin bags in succession and gently empty them into the acid, holding the bag close to the tub each time to avoid splashing.

The tub is half-full with body parts both wrapped and unwrapped. I take a moment to scan the horrific tableau. Thoughts of Raven and Buford's faces run through my mind and send a jutting shiver down my spine. In around 48 hours all that they were and all that they would ever have been will have dissolved into less than steam.

I slowly make my way towards the door, thinking how this nightmare will be over the next time I walk back through it. Does anyone ever truly walk off into the sunset, or is that horizon always flecked with memory's spatter of bloody misdeeds which we can't unspill?

My left hand slightly outstretched behind me, I gently close the basement door without looking back. The short walk up the stairs feels like a mountain trek to a now-fractured normality. This is a waiting game which I can't wait to finish.

All I want to do is go home.

CHAPTER 16

A watched pot never boils, while an unattended vat of sulphuric acid and loose body parts lingers constantly in the mind with veiled threats of disaster. I've been rooted to Raven's sofa for hours, trying and failing to focus on literally anything else. Mindless channel-hopping and staring at the walls can't shake this terrible thought. What if the body parts don't dissolve?

An assortment of burner phones in several colours is sprawled out on the glass table in front of me. Every beep and buzz sends a jolt of dread into my heart and stomach. I've not checked any of the messages. I'm too scared to. The called IDs and message alerts act as a glint of light through a creak in a door that needs to stay closed. So far, I've seen nothing that's obviously from Lola. I wonder if she's taken the same approach with the phones which she swiped.

I pick up a mauve phone and begin scrolling through the contacts. After several seconds I come across a WhatsApp group called 'THE GIRLS'. This gives me an idea.

'TOMORROW NIGHT. EVERYONE AT YOUR REGULAR POSTS. KEEP YOUR EYES AND EARS OPEN FOR ANYONE LOOKING FOR RAVEN.'

This way I won't have to scroll through hundreds of burner texts.

'ANY MONEY YOU MAKE IS YOURS AND YOURS ALONE.'

I write in capitals without thinking after seeing Raven's last several text messages. Immediately after hitting send, I place the phone back on the table. I don't dare to look at my watch. Not glanced at it since the basement. Time has inched by at an agonizingly glacial pace since the last of the remains hit the acid and looking at my watch isn't going to move it along any faster.

Sleep would be most welcome right now, but it could also make things worse. Every attempt to shift my mind towards literally anything else has failed beyond the immediate and momentary. What will happen when I surrender my thoughts completely and could I even if I wanted to?

For several minutes I blankly stare at the kitchen area, not sure at all what I'm looking for and less certain of what I will find. I walk across and open a cupboard door to the left of the oven before quickly slamming it shut. None of the contents register an impression on my mind. After a brief pause, I walk to the right of the oven and quickly open and shut two doors under the sink. Behind a third door I find a full bottle of Johnny Walker Red Label.

I grab the bottle in the palm of my right hand while, still crouched, holding the door open with my left. Scanning the label, I rise to my feet and casually flick the doors shut without looking.

'It must be five o'clock somewhere.'

A deep and sullen breath follows.

'Fuck it.'

My left hand reaches out for a cupboard door up above and opens it to reveal several shelves of glasses. A portly tumbler on the middle shelf catches my eye and I gently pull it towards me before placing it on the work surface. After closing the cupboard door, I unscrew the bottle and tilt it, ready to pour.

'Hah!'

Several seconds of hesitation pass until the glass fills up with liquid fire.

A rapid, violent pounding in the distance shakes me from a pitch black slumber. I'm laid out on Raven's king bed with no recollection of how I got there and just rusty fragments of what came before that. The last thing I can recall properly is setting up shop in the basement. My body is aching from head to toe, while a hard cloud pierces behind my eyes and temples.

The knocking continues while through a glazed view I stare at the bare white ceiling. Blurred, nondescript shapes tease me with hints of fuller visions as I tentatively raise my neck from the bed's surface. A whisky tumbler holding a swish of flat brown spirit rests in my right hand, its rancid scent offering no temptation at this early hour. Before me I can make out a DVD menu of *Scarface* on Raven's plasma screen. The strange thing is that I can't even remember watching it.

'Fuuu-uuu-ccc-k.'

This hammering is relentless and only serves to heighten the discomfort caused by my physical malaise. I can barely move a muscle in my body as a bubble of numbness cruelly envelops me. The walls on either side of me swivel and drift further back in keeping with the intensifying tingling in my legs and torso. My right hand tentatively creaks backwards and the fingers curve upon losing feeling, causing the glass to fall from my shaky grasp. Whisky stains the duvet cover, with a few errant drops rolling off the bed and onto the floor.

'OPEN THE FUCK UP!'

The banging goes on with me virtually immobile on the bed. I barely manage to lift my right shoulder off the surface, tilting my body at an awkward angle to the left. My torso frozen halfway between my intended move and a numbing reminder of my frailty, I turn my head all the way across in the hope that my body will follow. Following several seconds of tedious struggle, I creakily roll all the way around before falling off the bed with my hands in front of my chest. The fright of the fall bucks a sobering jolt through my chest.

'WE CAN DO THIS ALL DAY LONG!'

I'm sure they can.

'There's two ways we can do this, Raven.'

This doesn't feel much like the easy way to me.

'Shit.'

I eke back to my feet, temporarily allowing the bellowing from outside to powder out into form-bereft sounds. Upon turning around, I see the bedroom door. My limbs regain feeling with each passing second and forced movement. Without hesitation, I step forward and let myself out, sprinting towards the window directly opposite as soon as the door opens.

Looking down and out of the window, I see two men at the front door and a red El Camino parked in the driveway next to Raven's SUV. One man is white, one is black, and they both look like they're going to a funeral. I slowly open the window just slightly, careful enough not to make any kind of sound that might alarm the men in black. The convertible's red looks ominous, mirroring the bloodshed that I'm trying to forget.

'I'm glad we brought shotguns for this, Ordell' says the black gentleman. 'Yep' replies his white companion. 'Looks like we've got a biter on our hands, don't it? I tell you what, Vic, I'll take the backdoor. You man here out front and put in a call to Masuka.'

'Masuka?'

'Yeah.'

'Isn't that a little premature?'

'We just want her en route. It's better to have her standing by and not need her than need her and not have her standing by. Remember last time, with Arnie?'

'How could I forget? You didn't tell me you'd replaced the regular bullets with hollow points.'

'You didn't tell me you didn't know how to work the safety.'

'Alright, alright. Let's just do this, OK.'

'Fine.'

Vic and Ordell turn around and take a few short steps towards the boot of their car. After flipping the boot open, Vic pulls out two shotguns and passes the one in his right hand to Ordell. He slams the boot shut with his other hand and returns towards the front door. Ordell passes Vic on his left and walks around towards the back of the house.

'Shit.'

I catch Vic looking up out of the corner of his right eye and I swiftly back away from the window, leaning my back against the wall below. I'm unarmed and helpless. My plan to escape through the back is no more. Where would I have run to anyway? This isn't back home. I don't know these streets at all. I'll be damned if I'm going to call Lola and tell her that Plan B has failed. Besides, it's not safe to leave here, given what's still in the basement.

They say they can do this all day long, but how long will it be before they decide that they want to do more than just wait? I turn and crawl to my knees with my hands on the window sill, peeking down to see Vic still out front and glancing over to see the house across the road. The errant germ of an idea runs through my head while I crouch back down. Upon looking downwards, I notice the shape of a phone in my right jean pocket. It suddenly occurs to me that I should have brought my hazmat suit for this job. The messes are piling up further.

As fate would have it, I clocked the number on the front door of the house opposite this one. For some reason, a lone splash of red dirt which I spotted on the SUV door a few moments ago springs to the forefront of my mind. Come on Michael. Forget about it. Focus on doing what you need to do.

I'm going to call 911. I'll say I'm from that house across the road. There's a car across the way facing the house. There are two men sitting inside, loitering, flashing the headlights, drinking. Could always add loud music to the list of grievances. It's somehow serendipitous that Vic and Ordell reverse-parked so that their car is facing the house opposite. On the other hand, it gives them a shorter distance to walk back and retrieve their shotguns in front of less prying eyes if needs be.

Serendipity.

Bullshit.

Here's hoping that the Vegas cops are a little faster than the boys in blue back home. I once called them out after finding an unconscious man with a crack pipe in my building's hallway.

They never came.

'Yo Ordell, whaddya say we send someone over to the boyfriend's house? Bring Nile over in person? Sleeping beauty might rise and shine for a booty call.'

What?

'We can hang back in the car until he gets here. Yes, this is my way of subtly saying that I'm fucking bored out here. Actually, I'll hand in the car. You stay put.'

Already?

'Fuck me.'

Vic is getting antsy. Thankfully, they have no desire to kick down the door, saving the shock and awe for when they're inside. I need to call 911 now and hope that a patrol car gets here before Nile does. Nile has a key, and I haven't put the chain on the door this time. I can't risk Vic hearing me if I run downstairs. From where the car is seated, he'll hear the chain fastening. After all, Diana could hear Raven's phone ringing from exactly the same distance.

'Here goes nothing.'

I pull the phone out of my pocket and start dialling. It all comes down now to the good grace of chance.

CHAPTER 17

The torture of waiting. Moments seem like hours, dragging along tortuously with no end in sight. Nothing I say or do can move the anvil of the present any further down the line. Every gaze out of the window in the hope of seeing something that wasn't there the last time proves fruitless, so too does any attempt to divert my thoughts elsewhere even momentarily.

This is a stalemate of the worst kind, beyond which is but an unknown. Why have these men come for Raven, and what is their endgame? Will forcing them to retreat merely delay a dark certainty, and how would the discovery of Raven and Buford's bodies, or what's left of them, alter their plans? I'm in no mood to find out.

I look down to see Vic become more frustrated by the minute. His colleague is informing him over the phone that there is no sign of Nile at or around his home. Just before dialling 911, I had the wherewithal to drop call Nile from the burner of Raven's that's in my pocket and then send him a threatening text that he thinks is from Vic.

From what I can hear Nile is gone and so is his car. Looks like he's leaving Las Vegas. Vic is growing hostile towards whoever is on the other end of that phone, asking them if they searched the block with their eyes closed before ordering them to retrieve the cinder blocks from Nile's place. He's going to stay on the line while his colleague looks around.

Then what?

Warning Nile bought me some time, but Vic's rapidly hastening urgency has thrown hot water on those hourglass sands. With his mention of cinder blocks, we now know what the goons came for. Vic, Ordell and their mystery partner clearly had Nile pegged as Raven's trap queen. So much for the D.L. after all.

These streets watch and these streets talk. Right now, they're quietly taunting me with allusions to holes in the desert. How long before these loquacious streets breathe word to these hired guns of Raven's two associates, one with a British accent? The fact that they're looking for Raven means that it hasn't happened yet, but it's just a matter of time.

Vic has been silent for several minutes, listening in while his colleague presumably rummages through Nile's house. What they're looking for should be as easy to find as actual cinder blocks for old pros like these. Therefore, this won't take long. No sign of a cop car in the distance. So much for best laid plans.

I fiddle with the burner for several seconds and find a landline number for Nile. If I call it now, I can stall whoever is in Nile's house for a few minutes and keep Vic at bay as well. The thought has barely left my mind by the time I hit dial and the phone suddenly begins ringing.

Two rings.

Four rings.

Six rings.

Eight. Ten. Twelve. Fourteen. Sixteen.

Manufacturer's voicemail greeting. Generic and soulless, as always. I wait several seconds before calling again.

Two. Four. Six. Eight.

'Hey asshole!'

It's a start, but how long can I stall them for now?

'You forgotten how to answer the phone?'

I'm the one making the call, so no.

'I know it's you, Garcia! Where's the fucking stuff?'

I hang up. The hornet's nest has been batted. Now it's time to let the hornets loose to buzz.

'You want your stuff? I'll give you your stuff.'

I begin typing a text to send to Nile's landline. A few moments from now this goon and Vic, who I can only assume the goon has on speaker, will hear a robotic voice telling them what's what.

'NILE, IT'S ME. I FUCKED UP. WE GOTTA GET OUTTA HERE. GRAB THE COKE AND MEET ME AT D&G, NORTH OUTLET MALL. THE COKE IS IN THE FLOOR SAFE, MASTER BEDROOM. REMEMBER?'

In the absence of Las Vegas's finest, I'll have to drive the wolves from the door myself. The bait is on the line. Will they nibble?

'Come on.'

Vic, his right ear to the phone still, sits up from his slouched position, alert and alarmed. It looks like the Hail Mary has landed.

'Gotcha.'

A minute passes and Vic still hasn't put the key in the ignition.

'What are you waiting for?'

A nervous pause while the ambivalent hangman twiddles the noose. Vic tightens his grip on his shotgun with his left hand while continuing to listen intently. The sullen silence is suddenly broken by an innocuous beep from Raven's burner.

'AIN'T NO COKE HERE ASSHOLE. YOU'RE NOT RAVEN. WHO THE FUCK ARE YOU AND WHERE'S OUR FUCKING STUFF?'

'What?'

Before I've had a chance to process what's happened, a loud thrash of reggaeton rings from the burner. Vic turns his head over his left shoulder and looks up at the window, forcing me to instinctively duck and hide.

'Fuck me!'

I quickly turn off the phone, but at this point it's like trying to force a warm bullet back into the gun barrel. An aggressive rattle emanates from downstairs and repeats for a few seconds more. Vic's trying to jimmy the front door open. Before the opening of the door can kill the rattling, I spring into the bedroom and hide inside the rectangular linen box at the foot of the bed. I just about manage to awkwardly close the lid from inside as the front door sounds shut.

Pitch black greets my open eyes and blocks my ears to the erstwhile clear and present danger. I lay on my back looking up as though I were in a casket, coiled and poised should the need arise. With my right hand I pull the burner out of my pocket, checking that it's switched off before gently placing it between my legs.

In here all sounds beyond those from the immediate vicinity are reduced to less than whispers. Footsteps in the distance are indistinguishable from the shelled booing that rings in my ears. The clopping of shoes suddenly materialises right next to me without my noticing their approach. They grind to a halt just as quickly.

'Where did he go?'

'You tell me. You're the one who heard his phone ring.'

'I did. It came from that window over there. And I definitely saw the top of his head.'

'So, he's Batman?'

'You're a fucking riot, you know that.'

'I'm just saying…..'

'We came here to collect $1.5 million worth of heroin, which we do not have. If we had it, we'd be outta here and halfway back to Jeremy with the dope.
Meanwhile, you're standing here cracking jokes while the dope which we do not have is losing street value. I'm just saying.'

'Look…..'

'On top of that, we're on thin ice with Jeremy after the cops pounced on that last shipment we were supposed to collect. So whaddya say you go downstairs and look for the dope, while I take care of things up here?'

A muffled noise sounds twice in the distance.

'Shit. Five-O out front. We gotta split.'

After a brief flurry of shoes clopping against the floor, I hear what can only be the window sliding open followed by Vic and Ordell climbing out and dropping into the garden. They won't be back for a few days, figuring that the house is hot on account of Raven. By the time they come back I'll be gone, and so will all traces of Raven.

I emerge from the linen box and slam it shut behind me before pacing back towards the window. In front of the El Camino and Raven's SUV is a stationary cop car. Silent. Sirens not flashing. The old loiter and intimidate routine. Suddenly the door opens, and an imposing figure duly emerges.

'Redclay?'

But why?

She knows but she can't prove. As our new partner, Diana wants to keep her latest gravy train on the tracks. I'm not going to complain.

Diana methodically looks over the El Camino. Nice to see her earning that exorbitant cut. She turns around and fixes her attention on the SUV, crouching down and retrieving something from the underside of the vehicle with her right hand.

'A tracking device?'

I'll attribute this to Diana merely being fastidious. A good bad cop, so to speak.

'OK.'

For some reason Diana's eyes are now drawn to the splash of red dirt on the SUV, dirt which speaks unmistakably of Red Rock Canyon. She could spend all the time in the world there and she'd see no sign at all of the thing she knows but cannot prove. The GPS will show her that we got to the outskirts of the canyon but never went in.

Diana looks back at her car and then glances at the house.

'What are you doing?'

Her gaze of ice stays fixed on the window down below and then gently turns to the front door. How did the sight of the dirt turn her attention towards the house? Why isn't she putting her key in the ignition and making for Red Rock?

She rises to her feet with authority, still staring at the house. Her glare, even from my distant vantage point, is one of deadly intent. Redclay's posturing fills me with equal measures of alarm and confusion. Why would she be looking towards the house, unless she knew for sure that a certain something is or was behind that front door? After seeing the red dirt, why would she not race to Red Rock? And how could she possibly know anything?

Redclay is now approaching the front door. Either she knows and she heads straight for the basement, or she's fishing and she finds me, ready to pick holes in my associate story. What if she insists on a guided tour of my associate's house? If she finds neither the remains nor myself, she will just back away, confused even further.

I can only control one of those variables. In my infinite wisdom, and arrogance, I ditched the hazmat suit and all for Plan B. Diana can easily find my hairs, fibres and other DNA here with little more than a cursory look. The only thing I can do now is ensure that Redclay doesn't find me here and hope that prompts her to stop sniffing around.

CHAPTER 18

Often as a young boy I found myself underneath cars. For the most part it was to fetch a runaway football or skateboard. Sometimes, though, I ended up there with a friend or two during a game of hide and seek. And look at me now. The gravelly asphalt scratches my torso while I watch the foot of the front door from beneath the SUV, wondering what Diana has seen and what she will do about it.

The linen box was far too risky. A cop like Redclay and her ruthless avarice are not to be underestimated. That linen box is one of the first places she would look for a false bottom and a lucrative stash beneath it. Even when we cut our deal, she had a look in her eyes which betrayed her dismay at losing the two keys she's owed by Raven.

I find it hard to move or even breathe in the awkward and unforgiving crawl space. Already somewhat winded by the drop down from the window to the ground, not to mention the unconvincing dash to the SUV, the lack of give between the underside of the vehicle and the ground below feels all the more punishing.

A noose tightens in the pit of my stomach. Every passing moment during which that front door remains closed fills my mind with nefarious possibilities. I can't arch my neck enough to look towards the upstairs windows. There's no sign of light downstairs, and if Diana does wander into the basement, then I'll never know it from here.

That run from the front of the house to the underside of the car, especially after such a patchy landing, reminded me that I'm not as fast as I used to be. My days of fearlessly climbing over and sliding under fences to get to the ball are well and truly behind me. Knowing this makes me immediately second-guess an idea that's just come to me.

I see a small rock to my left, just inches away from the body of the car. If I'm quick enough on my feet, or my stomach to begin with, I can slide across to grab the rock and lob it through one of Diana's windows. While the alarm sounds, I can sneak into the house from the backyard and fasten the chain on the front door.

But what is there to stop Diana from returning and finding another way in? I'm hoping that a broken window will be enough of an emergency to force her away from here. It isn't a great plan, but it is a plan. Too many variables, though. How far is Dirty Diana from the front door? Can I make it to the back and in fast enough? How easy will it be to force a window open? And what has Diana seen already.

It's too risky by far. There has to be another way.

My own phone is in my other pocket. It's amazing that amid all the whisky-fuelled haziness and hours of punctured memories that I managed to do this one thing right. I awkwardly reach into my left trouser pocket and pull out the phone with my left hand before repeating this routine on my right. My phone's battery is at 1%. Will it stay alive long enough for me to look up Lola's number before I punch it into the burner?

My sweaty and awkward left digits slip and slide for several seconds before eventually opening up my contacts list. Lola. With my right thumb I start a fresh text and fluidly key in the number before typing.

'IT'S ME. CALL DIANA AND TELL HER TO MEET YOU AT TREASURE ISLAND. NOW.'

I realize just how inane this plan is in enough time to delete the draft. This is Raven's burner. One of many, but there's a chance Redclay's number will be on it. Taking no chances, I toggle down my contacts list towards Redclay. I start a fresh text and key in all but the last four digits of Redclay's number before my phone dies.

'Shit!'

4-5-9-3. Or was it 4-9-5-3? Maybe neither. Try every possible combination. Desperate times.

'GOT YOUR TWO KEYS. MEET ME AT TREASURE ISLAND. NOW.'

Will Diana buy it? There's an outside chance that she hasn't been to the basement yet, so maybe. I didn't take the heads out of the garbage bags, so she has no way of knowing for sure if one of the melting bodies is that of Raven if she has been down there. Raven is in a dangerous world, so they could just as easily be his enemies.

I hit send again before quickly turning off the burner. I'm not making the same mistake twice. The name of the game now is patience. Again. One Mississippi. Two Mississippi. Three Mississippi. And there it is, not a moment too soon.

Diana emerges from the house, one hand on the other while the other tightly clutches a pistol close to her waist. She looks around cautiously in all directions before stopping just past the doorstep. Her manner conveys the kind of suspicion that could only come from absolute certainty regarding Raven. Diana pulls out her phone and pushes once with her right thumb.

I can just faintly hear the voicemail greeting followed by a huff of frustration from Redclay. She duly returns to the inside of the house and slams the door shut behind her.

How can Redclay be so certain about Raven without having seen his now lifeless face? Or Buford's, for that matter. I'm confused. I just don't get it.

The beer bottle!

No wonder Redclay insisted on going to the cathouse. She had someone in the house while we were all together. Before we went to work on the bodies. Whoever was in there obviously sent Redclay photographic proof of Raven and Buford's demise, complete with faces. She knew what was in that basement long before she entered the house and came here to ensure that her leverage remained undisturbed. And I called her here.

'She knows everything.'

It's fruitless to continue hiding. Nothing I can do from here will make Redclay unsee what she's seen. She's holding a trump card now. Diana's undone our lie and can easily extract our DNA from the house, along with that of our victims. But if I take ownership of what we've done, I can turn her trump card into a joker.

I slide out from underneath the SUV on my right and push the ground with my palms to bring myself back to my feet. By some miracle, my glasses have stayed on my face. I briskly wipe my hands on the front of my shirt before slowly making my way towards the front door. A quick look through the peephole offers no glimpse of Diana. Without hesitation, I ring the doorbell with my right index finger.

The metallic shrill of the doorbell makes my heart skip. It keeps pounding while I try to stand firm. After the text message from Raven which she knew from the outset was a ruse, Diana will be on her guard. She won't do anything stupid. After all, we're partners. Then again, she is a cop who deals in drugs and bribes. Traditional logic doesn't apply so much.

As the door opens, I step forward before it can ride all the way back to reveal Diana, forcing her to hastily retreat when it does. She doesn't even have time to think about reaching for her gun. I slam the door behind me with a flick of my palm and then walk towards Diana. Forcing her hand with each step, she paces backwards as I move towards her and her right hand fumbles behind her back. Suddenly her stride is broken by a wall behind her. Diana now realizes that she doesn't have room to draw her gun and her hand drops back by her side.

'So, Officer, what brings you here?'

'It's Sergeant, and I was just about to ask you the same thing.'

'Okay, Sergeant. Why don't we head down to the basement? I'll show you what I've been doing.'

Redclay gives me a look of surprise, like a woman watching her ace in the hole fall through her fingers. If she knows that she can't scare us by leveraging our darkest secrets, we can take the upper hand in this complicated relationship. Diana is a formidable ally, and taking this particular knife from her hand will make her a less formidable adversary if things go south.'

'After you.'

I stand aside as Diana gets her back off the wall and walks past me to lead the way. We turn left towards the stairwell and head down with Diana just a few steps in front of me. She reaches the door and turns her head over her left shoulder to look at me, as though she is waiting for a cue. My face gives her nothing, and after several seconds of eery silence Diana turns her head away from me and finally opens the door.

A few steps later and Diana, upon seeing the tub and its contents, turns to me with a look of feigned surprise.

'Your friends with the El Camino?'

As if she doesn't know already.

'Raven. And Buford.'

Her eyes open wider in a comically exaggerated fashion.

'We had something of a disagreement. Purely business. Nothing personal. Lola and I wanted to buy his Treasure Island territory. He didn't want to sell, so we sold it for him.'

Diana glares calculatingly at me, as though she's torn between trying to find the kernel of untruth in my story and not being able to argue with the evidence behind her.

'And the El Camino?'

Twice now she's asked about it. She's worried and can't hide it.

'First you tell me why you're here.'

Redclay is taken aback.

'I was responding to a noise complaint.'

'Bullshit.'

She says nothing.

'A noise complaint from the house across the road? About the El Camino?'

A look I can't fully decipher engulfs Diana's face.

'I know all about it. I made that call.'

Genuine surprise now, mixed with confusion. Diana's eyes are dancing lightly, her mind contending with a whole host of questions. She likes to be in control. This has clearly unnerved the bad Sergeant and made her second-guess her being here.

'So why were you really here?'

An awkward pause.

'My two keys. My cash too.'

'We gave you sixty grand for that.'

'That's your money. I want what's coming to me from Raven.'

A terrible lie cloaked in the truth of her avarice.

'Why would you lie about that?'

'Why would you call the cops when you've got a dead pimp and his bodyguard melting in the basement?'

She's got me there. I was impetuous, and now she's making me pay.

'I take it those weren't friends of yours in the El Camino. Their car is here, but now they're not. Are they friends of Raven?'

How much do I really want to tell her?

'It's safe to say they didn't come over to Netflix and chill with their boy. I'm guessing they were pretty unhappy, as though they were expecting him.'

Something Nile said when he tried to call Raven just hit me. He told Raven to be ready for tomorrow. Is Raven such a screw-up that Nile can't trust him with a simple exchange? Raven has been making enemies among the bikers and likely can't afford another mistake.

'Expecting him?'

'Yes.'

She's on the hook and ready to bite. I'm going to slow the reel before appealing to her inherent greed.

'They were hereto pick up some H for some guy called Jeremy.'

'Jeremy Goldstein?'

'I don't know. Who's Jeremy Goldstein?'

'You have a lot to learn about Las Vegas.'

'Isn't that what we're paying you for?'

'No. You pay me to watch your ass, not wipe it. And right now, you're not paying me anything. Your lovely wife told me I had to audition. Speaking of which, where is it going down?'

'What do you mean?'

'Lola told me she was going to give me a corner to shut down, remember? Which one?'

Opportunity knocks. Let her in.

'Corners. Plural. You keep your ears to the street and find out what people know about this. If anyone knows anything about what really happened here, you shut it down.'

'How would anyone know?'

'I don't know. How would they?'

For a brief moment that granite exterior flakes ever so slightly. Diana is on the ropes but still swinging hard.

'If this was a dope deal then where's the dope? Where's the cash?'

She bought it.

'I've no idea. Vic and Ordell were just about to start looking for the dope before they split.'

'Vic and Ordell?'

'Yes. You know them?'

'Of course. They're Jeremy Goldstein's bagmen. Looks like Raven pissed up the wrong leg.'

I have no idea and she knows it. No need to play into that any further at this point.

'That's where you come in. You keep your ear to the street, starting tonight.'

'Tonight?'

'Yes. The girls are working Treasure Island tonight. All of them are going to have their ears pricked up and their eyes open for anyone looking for Raven. Your job is to watch their backs tonight. You're the enforcer.'

'I'm there. What time?'

'We'll let you know.'

'Fine.'

'Now what do you say we split and find that dope? After all, that is what you came for.'

CHAPTER 19

Over an hour and a half of searching turns up nothing that even remotely resembles dope. An accountant, a cop, two dead bodies and a missing pile of drugs. I'm pretty sure there's a joke there which I haven't thought of yet.

'There's no fucking dope!' rages Redclay with a real fervour.

'You said that already.'

'Got any bright ideas?'

'The bagmen had someone over at Nile's house. I managed to listen in a little before they split. No sign of Nile. No word on the drugs.'

'For all we know he took them with him.'

'Anyway, those aren't the two keys you're owed by Raven. Those are Jeremy Goldstein's drugs.'

I should have said that earlier and avoided a tedious search.

'I'm owed, and someone's going to pay.'

Redclay is relentless. I want her gone. How to get rid of her?

'What about the cash?'

'If this was a dope deal then there's got to be cash on hand. Let's check the car.'

'Oh please! This might be your first rodeo, but I've been to enough of these to know that the cash is never in the car. It's always nearby.'

Tony Montana was right.

'Come here.'

She summons me towards the living room window with her left hand. We both stare through the glass for over a minute, me rather aimlessly but Diana with a real sense of focus and purpose. Diana remains silent. I have no idea what we're supposed to be looking for.

'Right there. Do you see it?'

Er, no.

'That's it right there.'

Now I'm confused, which I convey with a vacant stare.

'Come on.'

Diana leads me outside and then out onto the road. She looks both ways, ahead and behind her before glancing back at me with a slight nod. I return the nod rather tentatively, being careful not to show any further signs of puzzlement. Redclay, impossibly cool and deft, crouches down and dislodges the drain crate cover before me. After sliding it to one side, she looks down and reaches in with her right arm to pull out a black gym bag. She carefully places the bag on the road and swiftly unzips it to reveal several neat, clean stacks of bills.

'How did you know?'

'I spent enough time playing marbles on drains as a kid to know that this crate cover was the wrong way around. The cash is never in the car. Rippers and runners always go for the car. They're greedy, but they're lazy too.'

'So, you gonna put it back?'

'I'm sorry, what?'

'The cash. Are you gonna put it back?'

'Why would I want to do that?'

'Because it's Goldstein's money.'

'I'm owed for two keys, so I'm going to take what's mine.'

'You're not worried about blowback?'

'Goldstein's bagmen left their car here. He'll just chalk this one up to their incompetence.'

'OK.'

'Anyway, you're the one who suggested that I look for the cash.'

In the hope of getting rid of you so that I can get back to presiding over my two slowly dissolving corpses.

'Right.'

'I just want my two keys' worth. The rest is yours.'

'No thanks.'

'You above a little drug money, Mr Whoremaster?'

Yes.

'No.'

'Then what's the problem?'

'We're going to be running a legitimate escort service. I don't want one red cent of drug money anywhere near the business. This has the potential to be something truly amazing and I want to keep it out of the hands of the FBI. I can clean the seed money, that's not a problem. It's just a little easier if the funds aren't totally rabid.'

'What about all your grand plans for pensions and healthcare?' she asks with a snicker and a scoff. She doesn't need to know everything.

'It's all under control. Don't worry about it.'

'I'm your partner, so I need to worry.'

'Junior partner, and legally speaking you won't even be that. Your weekly points and guarantee will get lost amongst miscellaneous expenses. Unofficially, we're paying you to watch our back, which you will do. Officially, you're no higher on the totem pole than the coffee filters for the office kitchen.'

Diana, clearly shocked, quietly exhales. She takes several stacks of cash out of the gym bag and stuffs them inside her jacket before quickly zipping it back up.

'Get that crate cover for me.'

'OK.'

I slide the cover back over the square hole in the ground. Diana rises back to her feet, clutching the gym bag's handles with her right hand, before walking back towards the El Camino with a real sense of deliberation in her step. She paces around to the trunk of the car and looks both ways before jimmying it open while the bag rests at her feet. I look on as the trunk abruptly slams shut and Diana re-emerges with a tyre iron gripped in her right palm.

Diana, now in front of the car, proceeds to smash the headlights in turn before pulling out her phone with her left hand and starting a call. After a few seconds of faint ringing, a quiet voice answers. Redclay's affect is tentative and monosyllabic at first, not registering in my memory. She places the tyre iron on the ground before kicking it across to me with her left foot. I can't hear what is being said over the clanging of the metal against the concrete. By the time I've returned to my feet after crouching down to retrieve the tyre iron, Diana has concluded her phone call.

'What am I supposed to do with this?'

'Call it collateral.'

'Collateral?'

'Yeah. You don't trust me fully. I can tell. Hopefully, this can change all that.'

'I don't understand.'

'This is the tyre iron I just swiped from Ordell and Vic's car, a car registered to Jeremy Goldstein. It has my prints on it. This implicates me.'

My expression tells her nothing and shows her even less.

'Wait, you thought I wouldn't see through your little bluff about you two being wired for sound the other night?'

Yes.

'Rookies. So cute.'

Cute. That's a new one.

'This here doesn't prove anything.'

'Exactly. But I want you to enjoy it all the same.'

What?

'That right there is the most leverage you will ever get on me. On the other hand, I can finger you and your old lady for a double murder.'

Hell hath no fury like a dirty cop scorned.

'You've got your assignment.'

'So I have. But in light of the fact that I've just saved your lives, I now consider that assignment completed.'

'Saved our lives? How do you figure?'

'The El Camino is going into impound. By the time it gets there, a wholesale quantity of heroin, much like the one Vic and Ordell came for, will magically materialize in the trunk right next to the money.'

'And?'

'Goldstein has eyes and ears all over the precinct. I'm going to make sure that they see and hear that the El Camino was picked up at McCarran.'

'Even though it wasn't.'

'Yes, rookie, even though it wasn't.'

Fucker.

'Once Goldstein thinks his two bagmen have tried to fuck him over, he'll have no reason to sniff around Raven's old business concerns looking for what he didn't get today. That includes yours.'

Diana says that last part as though she's waiting for an ovation of some kind.

'I'll put out BOLOs for those two fuckheads and you won't see them for dust. It's foolproof.'

She expects glee from the man she just blackmailed. Wow.

'Once the dope's in evidence, he has the front burner

under at least half a dozen cops at my shop to make it disappear. Everybody wins, and he fucks off until the end of time.'

I tell her nothing and show her even less.

'I think that calls for a bonus.'

'Whatever.'

Diana's thrown. Her face gives away just enough. I walk back towards the house and past Diana without looking at her. Not looking back, I flick the door closed behind me and return my thoughts to the basement.

I take a deep breath, turn around and open the door before stepping back out onto the doorstep.

'Hey Diana!'

Sergeant Redclay turns around and looks right at me.

'I got a nice message earlier on from the leader of the local Valkyries chapter. He's most appreciative of Raven's recent demise. Seems news travels fast on these streets here.'

'Bullshit.'

She's got me. But not for long.

'I bullshit you not.'

How do you bullshit a bullshitter?

'The whole chapter is very grateful, and their friends in Vegas PD will do anything to protect those who protected their interests.'

I look right into her eyes. She's bought it enough to at least mildly panic.

CHAPTER 20

Tuesday night. One last moonfall in this mausoleum of misdeeds, anxiously waiting for what was once menacing and threatening to be no more. By this time tomorrow a fate most final will have fallen upon Raven and Buford. A grisly end which, based on what Diana said, they've no doubt resigned others to. Are we balancing the karma books in their world, or merely opening a dangerous new ledger in ours? A ledger written in blood which will eventually be balanced by another gruesome entry much further down the line.

All the waiting has rendered me numb and restless. Attempts by my mind to will time along prove fruitless and bring nothing but further anxiety. I've not ventured back into the basement since Redclay was here, still fearful of seeing the bodies pretty much as they were before with no resolution in sight. I was too wired to notice any difference when Diana was here. There's nothing I can do now but sit on the sofa and wait.

Every phone on the table intermittently buzzes and rings, while my own and the burner which is now my designated business line elicit no sound at all. As a single man back home, I had a love-hate relationship with this kind of solitude. All alone in my flat, no voices but those emanating from my latest binge-watch obsession. A sweet, static crevice all of my own between the buzz of Friday evening's escape and the slow crawl of Monday blues. After streaming away half the day, that sweetness often turned bitter as I found myself rueing my multiple empty inboxes and longing for chaos to break the sullen monotony.

This time I'm a prisoner to the chaos that came before, and this silence forms the bars between now and sweet relief. Is this all that life is, regardless of the choices we make: fleeting ebbs that break up the ongoing tempest, where we find ourselves being freed by or freed from the tumult?

The girls are working over their Treasure Island patch, keeping their eyes and ears wide open for anyone looking for their old boss. All I need is a slither of someone, anyone buying into Redclay's ruse. No word so far in either direction. Can any good come from checking in for a status update? An answer either way would end the torture of not knowing, while possibly shaking new dangers from the distant shadows into the light. No answer at all would merely prolong the agonizing stalemate and set my teeth even further on edge.

Redclay is there too, playing the role of the dutiful enforcer while keeping a potentially deadly fate in her back pocket. With one hand she spares us, and with the other she playfully wields the knife, knowing she can cut the strings whenever she wants. I showed her what she had already seen, as a means to show her that she can't frighten us by leveraging what she knows about Raven and Buford's murders.

Sure, she may not have fully bought that line of crap about the bikers, but at the same time she doesn't want to go further down that rabbit hole lest it should be proven true. It's a bluff she doesn't want to call, but I don't want to take the chance that she will.

Lola has tucked in Jennifer and called it an early night. In this cruel damask of iniquity, the love I feel for them is the burning lamp that will lead me to safety. Lola has given me something I'd never known before. For so long I was an ambivalent lone wolf, waking every day before the dull slack tide between dusk's last and dawn's first. Springing out of bed while the new day was still under the shadow of the one that came before. Just to flee the chill of a lonely bed.

Those creaking hours between three and six always brought me a strange sense of bliss. Behind closed blinds I felt like I was all alone in the world. A feeling so at odds with what would come for eight to ten hours later on. During that ceasefire between the tedium of the daily grind and my longing for something more, I found joy in the written word and my YouTube playlist.

During any given week I would alternate my pre-mornings between writing poetry, reading, the night before's WWE and Box Set City. A world of morally ambiguous, take-charge antiheroes who took what they wanted and answered to nobody but themselves. I often looked at these men and wondered if they had some kind of magic gene which I was missing.

I got nutty with McNulty. Drunk with Draper. Watched Pinkman & White launder ill-gotten paper. Got made with *The Sopranos*. Dished death with *Dexter*. Each extra episode in defiance of my best friend's lecture.

Those exact words formed the beginning of a wonderfully self-effacing poem which I wrote several months ago. The story ends with me heeding Andre's advice, stepping away from the frequent weekend-long binge-watch sessions, stepping out into the world and finding love. Balance too. As I wrote those words, I'd just started going out more in the hope of finding something special.

At seven every morning I would leave the flat and set sail for Southbury. The same four-train journey every single day, reading and trying to steal extra sleep. Every now and then the peace and quiet would be broken up by Freddie, a would-be preacher on the Barking to Gospel Oak train. He would sing about glory to God in the highest while boarding before launching into a sermon. These diatribes elicited sniggers, confused looks, shaking heads and, mainly, silence.

As the last leg of the journey loomed around the dull and dreary vistas of Edmonton Green, I slowly began to slip into character. Next stop: Boredom. Hours on end meandering through largely superficial social interactions and trying to avoid tedious conversations about things for which I could not care less. *Love Island*. *Fifty Shades*. *EastEnders*. Around the saddos in Accounts Payable I don't feel so abnormal and embarrassed for being a wrestling fan.

Those Tuesday night detours to Covent Garden always felt like walking through a portal into another world. One in which I don't feel like an outsider. A place where kindred spirits and outliers can come and just be, united in their love of a beautiful literary form which has sadly been relegated to the periphery in favour of the more vacuous and asinine.

After every show I would get home late and make myself a fish finger sandwich. While burning off the last of the adrenaline from my earlier performance in the first of the midnight oil, I would quietly reflect and wish that every single day could be more like Tuesday.

In some twisted way, I guess I am living out the ending of that poem.

Writer's block. The absolute worst. When the day-to-day of what an incredible young lady called boring adult life brings no joy, which is quite often, the written word always brings me solace and glee. Just me, my black rollerball gel ink pen, and several fresh sheets of paper, blank but for the grey lines that run across from top to bottom. Each fresh sheet of virgin, untouched A5 is a blank canvas of untapped possibilities. The clean spaces between the lines call out to me, a sacred call that only I can hear and only I can answer.

I feel like I'm mastering a domain which is mine and mine alone as I watch fresh words drip from the needle-like tip of my pen onto that page. Words of all kinds, from the esoteric to the ridiculous and everything in between, pour from my mind via the conduit of the pen. These words from the minutiae of other worlds, other lives, and bring me a strange yet sweet form of catharsis.

It's an otherwise ordinary Saturday afternoon. A gently undemanding Netflix dramedy provides the coddling background noise while I play a waiting game which I don't seem to be able to win. The blank page stares back at me on the sofa, teasing me with a sullen sense of expectation while inspiration eludes me. When these dry spells come, those words of old look like they were written by somebody else, and a page looks like a tough mountain to climb.

I write because life is crap, and at times like this I wonder if I can't write because life is crap or if life is crap because I can't write. Imagine fleeing towards the warmth of a benevolent mistress and finding that she's gone. No warning, no word of farewell and, worse still, even less of a clue as to whether or not she will ever return.

When my pen grazes the page, I'm in another world. It's like I'm able to say all the things that are in my soul, things which I don't get to say to anyone else. The ink paints my vision with colours of a life wholly unlike the one it grants me sweet escapism from. Conversely, when I stare at the blank page and inspiration doesn't look back, it might as well be any other day of the week, with me watching the clock and wishing it would end.

Every now and then, when the four walls begin to breed nothing but tedium and unkind reminders, I stepped outside and jumped on either the 174 or 175. Romford on a Saturday night. All those bars, all those clubs, the lights, the music, the girls. All making promises of unbridled fun and joy.

Get a drink. Get a table in the corner. Enjoy the music. Survey the crowd. Evade all attention. Blend into the walls. Leave. Rinse. Repeat.

Life passes by while you're waiting for something amazing that will never happen.

Life passes by just waiting for things to happen. Right now, I'm slowly passing the hours while the events of yesterday duly unhappen. Twenty-four hours from now, give or take, and all that will remain of our deadly secret is a dull, grey pool of acid. The memory will live on, but, with no physical reminder and the continuing flow of time, it will eventually recede into the ether of half-formed recollections. Given enough time, it will barely be distinguishable from the millions of dreams which mean everything in their immediate aftermath but, for the most part, are soon forgotten.

Angels so often find refuge in villainy, but does the demon's fall from the grace of wickedness ever end in anything but tragedy?

I begin walking listlessly around the house, looking for something, anything to silence the second-guessing. Anything but another shot at the late Raven's whisky. I'm not making that mistake again. After ditching Redclay, I spent a good half hour in the bathroom vomiting profusely. At one point I thought my vital organs were going to start coming up.

After dragging myself up the stairs, I open a door to my left and upon looking inside I see a computer. I step forward and tap the power key before being greeted by several open web browser tabs. Most of them contain porn. What a surprise.

Raven's computer is perfect for Operation: Seed Money. The IP address of a dead drug dealer's house in Vegas, assuming that I don't scramble the IPA, will leave Raj with even more awkward questions which he can't answer. Velma too. Better scramble the IPA. No need to lead anyone to our crime scene. Besides, Raj and Velma will be in enough trouble once this has been done.

And we'll be rich.

CHAPTER 21

'This entire trip has been a disaster. I just want to go home.'

These are the last words I remember saying last night before crashing to sleep. I said them while staring at the door of the basement room and thinking about what's on the other side. Operation: Seed Money couldn't stop the second-guessing. It only slowed it down temporarily. For all the good it did in that regard, I might as well having been watching Penn & Teller live from the nosebleed seats while fighting severe constipation.

Typical me. That's what it is. I can be wildly euphoric one moment, riding a glorious wave of golden fire and then all it takes is for an errant piece of debris to fly into the flames before everything grinds to a halt. Suddenly my overblown sense of joy turns into an all-encompassing cloud of the most morose variety. When it comes, I can no longer see the burning wave, only the debris, and all memory of what came before has been vanquished.

This dangerous foible of mine, this kind of all or nothing, black and white thinking has cause myself and others, including my doctor friend Waqas, to suspect that I have BPD or bipolar. In addition to my anxiety, high-functioning autism and OCD. That's quite a collection. In all seriousness, that complete loss of perspective when something goes just slightly wrong is far from normal. I always come to in the cold light of day and end up hating myself for having been such a fool before.

For once I may have been right. None of those previous instances involved dead bodies in a tub of piping hot acid. Never have I felt that fear and foreboding quite like I did yesterday. A terrifying sense of walking tightrope on the edge of the sun and knowing full well that at any moment you could fall into the fury of the fire. A part of you wishes that you would, simply to end the teetering dread of the inevitable fall.

After all of yesterday's turmoil, a strangely peaceful sleep followed. The kind enjoyed by a condemned man who has accepted his fate and let his guard down. From around 11:30 last night to shortly after midday, the hours passed in a blur of black without so much as a lingering hint of a dream. Upon waking up I felt strangely unburdened. The sun is shining a little brighter than it did a day ago and I am just hours away from sweet relief.

I slowly roll off my back and sit up on the couch before checking my phone. A message from Lola which reads

'I love you Bunny x' brings a smile to my face. For a few moments I stop and stare at the screen, forgetting everything else and embracing the warm feeling in my heart. Like a bright crimson rose in full bloom amid the carnage, it reminds me that everything will be OK.

'Love you too Pussycat x' reads my reply. I scroll through the WhatsApp group to check in with the girls. No word of anyone sniffing around looking for Raven. Everyone clocked out at six in the morning as planned, each girl dropping a quick 'I'm out' with a smiley face. Every girl except for Honey. It's fast approaching 12:30 and I'm trying not to read anything into it.

Any thought that something could be wrong leaves my mind just as quickly as it entered. For the most part I attribute it to my typical overthinking, but on some selfish level I don't want anything to disrupt this new sense of peace. Not just yet.

I begin scrolling through my contacts list and suddenly land on Raj's number. A smug smile engulfs my face as I think about this overbearing narcissist and how he has no idea what's about to hit him. I'm just sorry that I won't be there to watch the silver bullet take flight. The wicked are often happiest while sitting obliviously in the line of karma's fire, just before the killer blow lands.

A goofball impulse takes hold of me and all I can think of is *Take This Job & Shove It*. I put the phone back down on the table, stand up and leave the room, setting my sights on the stairs and my mind on the computer up there. Once I arrive, I seat myself and begin composing a pipe bomb of an e-mail. An eloquent yet explosive diatribe which I've recited almost word for word in my head over the last several months.

To: Raj.Panesar@RegalWorldwide.com

Bcc: LONDONALL@RegalWorldwide.com

From: michaelosullivan2018@gmail.com

Subject: Tomorrow

Now that the formalities are out of the way, it's time to make Raj eat shit and like the taste of it.

Dear Raj,

Hope you're well.

Ahead of my scheduled return to work this Thursday, I would like to inform you that I am leaving the business with immediate effect. No gardening leave. No PILON. None of that will be necessary. I just want to leave now, please and thank you.

I'm leaving Regal because I can't stand to be around you for another minute. Just like Janet couldn't. Just like Priti couldn't. Just like Pawlina couldn't. Just like Amjad couldn't. Just like Tanveer couldn't. Please, be kind enough to let me know if I've missed one.

You're probably wondering why everybody hates you, given that you're such a benevolent and gracious man. First of all, there's that awful toupee on your head. Whoever sold it to you has a wonderful sense of humour. It looks like Pepe Le Pew's corpse up there. What happened? Did Burt Reynolds have a jumble sale?

Then there's your personality. Never in my life have I seen such a jumbled mass of insecurity and negative energy. You're 'In it to win it' speeches? No. Just no. That's all.

What you said to Priti about how Credit Control suits her because she's a girl was just disgusting. You say that accountancy is only for men. You're so incredibly enlightened. It's amazing.

Then there're that £75,000 black hole where your corporate card receipts should be. That said, I can fully understand where you're coming from. Nobody wants to be that guy in the casino or strip club asking for a receipt.

Apart from all that, you're a great man. You truly are, and I wish you nothing but the best in all of your future endeavours.

Best Regards,

Michael O'Sullivan

I take a moment to stop, smell the roses and admire my deliciously acerbic masterpiece. My right index finger hovers over the ENTER key while the cursor is placed firmly over Send. A strange twitch takes over my finger and spreads to the rest of the digits on my right hand while I continue staring at the words on the screen.

As soon as I hit Send, the door will firmly slam shut on my old life back in London. The days of being an insecure doormat, so unsure of myself and wishing I was somebody else. No more three in the morning starts, sleepwalking through tedious train rides to a job that I hate, day after day of ghosting through office hours, just to get to a weekend that ends with me trying in vain to hold back the waning Sunday hours and keep reality at bay just a little longer.

Isn't it funny? We spend so long pining for something else, not always something in particular, yet when it's so close that one step will not only take us there but put an infinite distance between us and the thing we were running from, we hesitate. Is it that infinite distance behind us that we fear? Do we become so used to running and longing that we can't imagine anything else? After looking for something, anything, to take us away from our current reality, do we encounter a new kind of uncertainty when faced with one particular something, wondering if it's really what we wanted?

It's amazing how one small action or inaction can change the course of fate in such indelible ways. The angry would-be gunman oversleeps through his rage with his piece and his kill list under his pillow, missing his window of opportunity. His murderous machinations are reduced to a fleeting flurry of red mist which only he will know about. No headlines on the six o'clock news. No bloodshed. No tragedy. Nothing.

I love Lola. We have this deep connection, already, and she understands me like nobody else ever has. Friday night going into Saturday morning was the most magical time of my life. After the wedding we stayed up all night, making love, watching *The Wolf of Wall Street*, listening to Sade and Prince and, most of all, talking and laughing.

Lola is unlike anyone I've ever met. She has a unique spirit and such vast intellectual curiosity. I feel like we're two outliers, gleefully skirting the periphery of convention. I knew right away from looking at Lola that she was one of the sweet ones, the kind ones, and also, for better or worse, that she wasn't like the others. Having felt so fundamentally different from other people for so long, I have a strong sense in this regard.

Like myself, she's not one for selfies and social media. We talk about *The Picture of Dorian Gray*, *Brave New World* and *1984*, laugh at bad movie and book reviews on YouTube, listen to egregious song lyrics and jokingly replace them with politically correct alternatives and talk about anything and everything. Poetry, psychology, life. Everything.

I never thought a woman would ever write me a poem.

A cynical voice asks if this is really love. I've never felt love before, so how would I know what it looks like? Am I just a deluded fool, latching onto the first thing that even remotely resembles a meaningful romantic connection, fearful that if I don't, it will never come around again?

Sometimes I feel like I made Lola up and sooner or later she will leave me.

The last time I listened to and followed such a voice, ironically, I grabbed what came first while there was something much greater in the foreground. I spent years regretting it and wondering what could have been if I'd walked away from Regal just weeks after starting to embark on a career in investment banking. But today is a new day, yes, it is. A new day, one in which I trust my instincts and bet on myself.

Send.

CHAPTER 22

The moon. A beacon of otherworldly hope lighting up the sky as the old day slowly folds while making quiet promises for the next one. Like a lone pearl dropped into an ocean of damask. A flotilla of clouds both black and white wash over it from right to left, the former briefly obscuring the lunar majesty while other clouds lap to it like waves of spent smoke.

We stood together, Lola, Jennifer, and I, looking up at the moon and sharing a beautiful silence. A silence betraying an ebullient glee which did not speak at that moment. I feel warmth and true earnest affection for my new wife and stepdaughter. This feeling depletes the dying whisper of the notion that our marriage was merely a hotshot response to a primitive urge, one with permanent ramifications.

Sure, maybe it was just that to begin with. A deadly manifestation of my longing for something I've never felt before. On Friday morning Lola gave me something amazing. She wasn't my first good time girl, and even if she had been, it went far beyond that. When I saw her at the bar that night, I took it as a sign of something deeper. I knew after that I would likely never see her again unless I acted, so I rolled the dice in the dark. Decided to take whatever comes next. At the very least, I would go back to the boys with a funny story for the ages.

The chemistry came at the bar that morning. The love kicked in during the hours that followed our vows. Just as I knew and hoped it would. In a town where most people bet big on the turn of a single card or one spin of a wheel, a beautiful stripper I'd met less than a day ago seemed like a safe bet.

That slow and deliberate procession of the clouds across the moon's face mimicked, at least in my memory's eye, my pouring of the dull acid graveyard down the drain just hours ago. I stood by and watched the grey liquid slide through the gaps in the gutter, while a benevolent sun slowly dissipated any overflow which had stuck to the grate covering. Just like that, our deadly mistake was gone.

From the terror of that moment, and all that precipitated it, to the tenderness of this one, life sure has been strange lately. In the jaws of the lowest lulls, we can see nothing beyond the present darkness. Not even the inevitable aftermath, for when the fire engulfs us with no sign of anything else, we've long conceded that it's already over. In the glow of the calm which eventually follows, the one which looked like it would never come, the feeling is similar. Except in the rapture of that momentary joy we can't see beyond the blue sky right in front of us. Nor can we imagine another hell like the one we've just fled.

Life is a succession of these swings and roundabouts, and in the dangerous world I now inhabit with my new family I can't afford to mistake a fleeting reprieve for total absolution. That said, these sweet moments should be savoured and enjoyed. The promise of many more just like it is all the reason I need to persevere. Even if the road to each sunset goes through an ocean of thumbtacks and razor wire.

In the name of survival, I will walk down that road again and again. Ashes are all that remain of that bridge back to the humdrum life I put on hold for this Stateside sojourn. Before me is a new path, one which I won't walk alone but instead saunter through hand in hand with a great love I never saw coming.

'Tell me, Jennifer, what do you see when you look at the moon?' Jennifer looks back at me with a luminous smile and an unmistakable sense of youthful wonderment.

'I see a big ball of cheese.' Her words, alive with all the joys of young imagination, touch a hitherto unscathed corner of my psyche and are enough to make my heart melt. I've never been particularly paternalistic before, but in this very moment I can feel something I've never felt before. I look at Lola and silently smile before turning and shining that same beam onto Jennifer.

'You're right. It is a big ball of cheese. What if we were to take a rocket out there, all three of us, and start eating the cheese? Everybody on Earth would be looking up and saying 'Look, there's a piece of the moon missing! How cool would that be?'

'Yay, yay. I wanna go. I wanna go. Mummy, can we? Can we?'

'Can we?' chimes Lola, gleefully.

'Of course we can. But first I have to let you in on a little secret.' I slowly crouch down beside Jennifer and move my mouth level with her ear.

'You see those shadows on the face of the moon?' Jennifer nods excitedly.

'Those are the shapes of the countries that are without the moon right now. When they look up, they can see the sun. Tomorrow when we see the sun, they'll look up and say 'Look, it's America's shadow'.'

'Wow!'

'It's true. That's why we have to be careful when we eat the cheese. You see that shape there?'

'Yeah.'

'That's England. That's where Daddy's from. You have to eat around the shadows or England will disappear and King Charles will be in your tummy forever!'

Lola smiles a beaming megawatt smile, sharing in her daughter's joy.'

'If King Charles is in my tummy, will that make me a queen?'

'You are already a princess, and one day you will be a queen just like Mummy.'

'A princess like Moana?'

'Better than Moana.'

Jennifer's face radiates a halcyon warmth which burns bright in her young eyes. I look to Lola, and she looks back at me. Our eyes lock and we share a sweet stir of contentment. We're bound. Not just by our words and vows, or the nascent love that continues to grow, but by all that we've been through over the last few days. We share a secret, we've seen one another do things which those who have known us for years could never imagine. We are two steeds way out in front of the pack, fighting a war that the rest will never even see.

This moon glistens in my eyes like a brand new emanation. No longer a harbinger of days of same, mere stretches of daylight which play out just like and are completely indistinguishable from all those that came before it. The last week has been like a wild ride on the other side of a forbidden door, a door which recedes into the distance like a faraway homeland while the new atmosphere engulfs me to become the new normal.

Part of me, driven by reason and logic, thought and talked about running amid the chaos and carnage. A greater part of me, steered by viscera and the emptiness in my heart which I felt as I boarded the plane from Heathrow to San Francisco two weeks ago, had no such intention. Through all the fear and uncertainty of anything but tragedy, I felt a strange rush of adrenaline. At first it was as though I was gliding through someone else's life, mainlining a vicarious thrill. After emerging from the flames just slightly singed, I was truly awake.

During the drive home with Lola from Raven's house, I felt an indescribable lightness in my heart. A heart no longer weighed down by an unrequited sense of desire and jealous curiosity regarding all that existed beyond the fence of a life more ordinary. Through the silence I felt a closeness to Lola that was beyond all that words could bring.

All that remains of what we did is the plastic tub which held Raven and Buford's remains less than an hour ago. It's now nestled safely in the trunk of the car, wiped clean of all debris left behind by our sins.

Are we any different from anyone else, in that we go to work, do our job, pack up and go home to be with the ones we love? The working stiffs, of whom I was one, who die inside for 40 hours a week. Pretending to care about a litany of meaningless spreadsheets and reports, just so that they can scrape a tiny share of what they put in the pockets of faceless moguls who don't know they're alive.

We are different. Different in that we took control of our destiny. Did the things that they can only do in their darkest dreams. Dark dreams which grow ever darker the longer their suffering goes on. Are we all just demons when it comes down to it, hiding behind masks of respectability because we fear what we're truly capable of? Not to mention what we deserve.

What we have goes far beyond love and respect. We are two soldiers bonded by battle who know things about one another that not another soul does. Kindred spirits existing outside the margins of what and who we're told we should be.

On the way home Lola insists on taking a detour and heading to the Treasure Island Starbucks. Sure, there are many other places closer to home where we could have grabbed a coffee, but Lola says there's something about the way her friend Amy makes coffee. She's not shy in telling Amy this. I'm sure Amy gets tired of hearing how good her coffee is.

While sipping my large cappuccino, I look out upon the strip and recall how this time last week I was on the outside looking in at someone sitting in this exact spot. Looking out from behind the window, at every bright light, every flash of neon and colour, every gleam of a passing sportscar and sharp-suited passer-by, I see opportunity.

This city is ours for the taking.

CHAPTER 23

After dropping Jennifer off at pre-school, Lola and I head to Denny's for breakfast. I take the steak and eggs with a side of buttermilk pancakes, while Lola has French toast with some chocolate-dipped strawberries. A handsome and amiable middle-aged waitress of East Asian appearance refills our cups with black coffee while the stereo gently beats out some Coldplay.

'This is our song. Your song. From our wedding. Whenever I hear this, I think about you coming through that door and down the aisle towards me. You know, for a second there when I was standing next to the minister, I thought you were going to get cold feet and run away.'

'Not a chance.'

Lola brushes some errant hairs out of ger face with her left hand before sliding her right across the table and placing it on top of mine. She tenderly squeezes my wrist and looks into my eyes with a warm, stirring glow. Our eyes meet and Lola gives a gentle tilt of her head to the left.

'Not…. a…. chance.'

'Wow!'

'Tell me, why would I?'

'I don't know. Why would you?'

'Are you kidding? You're the first man who's ever truly made me feel like I'm worth more, more than a quick fuck in the parking lot of White Castle. You're the first man to ever buy me flowers, bring me chocolates. Hell, you write me poems. And I never thought anyone would ever want to marry me.'

'What? Nobody ever gave you flowers? Not even Jennifer's dad?'

'Jennifer's dad? No way!'

'I thought you said he took you to the theatre and all that.'

'Er, yeah. He did. He just never bought me flowers. Didn't like them.'

Weird.

'Weird.'

'It was what it was.'

'You deserve all the flowers in the world, and I'm going to give them to you.'

She smiles and gives my wrist another, more playful squeeze. Though something sits a little crooked in my mind, I feel more or less at ease during the quiet pause. Lola's phone suddenly pings and abruptly shakes us out of our moment. Before Lola can reach her phone, it emits several more rapid-fire pings.

'Shit. The group chat is blowing up big time.'

'What's up?'

'It's Honey. She hasn't been home since her shift on Tuesday night. None of the other girls have heard a word from her since.

'Check her individual WhatsApp. When was she last online?'

Lola toggles on the keypad with her thumb for several seconds before responding.

'Not a peep since 5:24 yesterday. A whole half hour and change before she was supposed to check in.'

My heart drops like a silent anvil falling into the pit of my stomach. Is this how avarice works? Spreading like a raging fire which will stop at nothing until the entire forest is asunder, and all that remains is you standing over an empire of ashes. The ashes of the just and the unjust alike, cruelly marking the wages of vice and all that they buy.

There can be no more bloodshed. Except in the name of survival. Raven and Buford happened as it did, and there's nothing that can be done it about it. But Honey? This isn't right. She doesn't deserve this. Not one bit.

Honey was just out there doing her job, and at my behest. I sent her out there as a pawn, to gauge the danger for Lola and I, and in the process, she's been burned by the very flames she went out there to survey. If anything has happened to Honey, her blood is on our hands.

But why?

'We need to call Redclay' I blurt.

'Redclay? But why?'

'I saw the look in Redclay's eyes after her altercation with Honey back at the sorority house.'

'It's not a sorority house.'

'Whatever. Anyway, you can't put this past Redclay. She likes to be in control and will do whatever it takes to show us who's in charge.'

'Where are you getting this from?'

The GPS on Raven's car, the search team she sent to the house, whatever photos they took of the bodies....

'It's just a hunch.'

'We don't have time for hunches right now. Besides, it doesn't make sense.'

I decide to let it go. Just as well, given that I've not told Lola that whoever was at the house was there at Diana's behest. This is neither the time nor the place for that difficult conversation, especially with Honey's life hanging in the balance.

'Diana can help us. Firstly, she can confirm whether or not Honey is in police custody.'

'You don't think she'd have told us by now?'

'I'm going to ask her anyway.'

Lola, with the digits on her right hand, quickly flicks at the phone keypad some more before holding the device to her right ear.

'What are you doing?'

'I'm calling Honey without the caller I.D. this time. If someone has her, they'll be anxious to know who's looking for her.'

I overhear seven pairs of faint rings before the line suddenly goes dead. Lola furiously taps several more buttons before showing me the phone screen.

'I KNOW WHERE YOU ARE. I'M EN ROUTE. SEE YOU IN FIFTEEN.'

'Consider the hornet's nest batted' Lola exclaims.

'What now?'

'They'll call back. Just give them a minute to finish shitting their pants.'

I'm more than slightly unnerved by Lola's confidence in the face of such a terrifying situation. Several seconds of silence pass, during which I can do nothing but nervously shuffle my fingers and look around. Lola is unmoved, poised even, as the tense seconds turn into a minute and that minute into two.

The silence is broken by the jarring rattle of the phone's buzz. Lola allows it to ring twice more before answering, saying nothing but listening intently. I can't make out many of the words being growled at the other end, but I notice a swift and marked change in Lola's expression during a break in the one-side conversation.

CHAPTER 24

Lola and I are standing outside the entrance of Flamingo waiting for Redclay to arrive. My wife is already visibly incensed, and Diana is running late, which sets her even further on edge. The Strip is abuzz with passers-by in all directions and the playful pinging chimes of games machines, while a scent of sweet synthetic vanilla clings to the morning air.

'I'll do the talking, OK Lola?'

'Right. Like you did with Raven? This time why don't you tie yourself to a chair first, pre-empt the inevitable?'

'I was getting somewhere with Raven before you burst in and -.'

I remember where we are and suddenly stop myself before stealing a deep and calming breath.

'Look, you going in all guns blazing, hurling accusations, won't help matters. Let's hear Diana out. There might be a perfectly logical explanation for this, one which will help is to get Honey back much faster.'

'I don't need to know all the ins and outs of why she fucked us over. I just want to get Honey back.'

'We need to tread carefully here.'

'Why? Why do we need to tread carefully? Do I need to remind you that a woman's life is on the line here?'

No. But I need to tell you that Diana has pictures of our crime scene. Not now. Later.

'Is there something you're not telling me? Michael?'

'That's funny. I should be asking you that.'

'What's that supposed to mean?'

'Well, -.'

We stare awkwardly at one another for several seconds, oblivious to everything else. Lola lightly exhales, waiting for me to say something. But I can't. My mouth opens before freezing, like a half-cocked hammer on a pistol. I can't bring myself to say the words.

'Get in.'

The voice to my left and Lola's right startles me. It's Diana pulling up in a black Dodge Charger. Lola gets in the back through the door nearest to us. I wait for her to slide over so I can get in, but she buckles her seatbelt without even looking at me. For a brief moment I shake my head before walking around the rear of the car and entering on the other side.

'So, ladies, what seems to be the problem?'

This is no time for jokes. I extend my left hand to signal to Lola.

'Honey's missing. She's been kidnapped by Goldstein's men, on account of the drugs found in Vic and Ordell's car.'

'Who's Honey?'

'You cannot be fucking serious!' snaps an indignant Lola.

'Goldstein wanted Raven's dope, so I gave him Raven's dope.'

'You what?' I reply, my tones injecting a drop of London into this sea of American twang.

'I called in a favour from a friend at the Clark County Sheriff's department. About a year ago he sized a similar sized load from these Juggalos who thought they were big time. They wouldn't snitch, but I know they got the drugs from Raven.'

'Cute fucking story.' Lola is becoming more and more agitated by the minute.

'So, what's the problem?'

'The problem, Princess Di, is that the heroin which is now in Goldstein's possession is laced with fentanyl.'

'Like I said, he wanted Raven's drugs, he got Raven's drugs. Raven sells shit, so that's what he got.'

'Yes, and he's not too happy with the quality of the merchandise' I reply. 'Apparently he was expecting pure uncut heroin.'

'From Raven? Really?'

'As much as I'd love to continue this conversation about heroin quality, we've got a situation here. Honey will die if we don't act fast.'

'Tell me again, who's Honey?'

'YOU SAY THAT ONE MORE TIME AND I WILL FUCKING KILL YOU!'

Lola's outburst gives me chills and leaves me genuinely stunned. By contrast, Diana is totally unshaken, like a seasoned gunfighter who has stared down many a barrel. I see the reflection of her cold brown eyes in the rear view mirror as the atmosphere in the car drops like a stone.

Diana looks down and duly turns on the car stereo, which begins playing nondescript 1980s power rock.

'So, we have a dissatisfied customer.'

'Yes, you could say that.' My forced diplomacy is beginning to wear thin.

'I don't know what Goldstein's problem is. He got what he wanted and more.'

'Including one of our girls.'

'Oh, Honey. I remember now.'

Lola shakes her head but says nothing. I echo her sentiments internally. Upon looking forward at Diana, I see a hint of a menacing smirk.

'Now that you remember who Honey is, what do you suggest we do in terms of getting her back? Goldstein is unhappy with Raven, which, given Raven's current condition, means that we have a problem. Raven hurt Goldstein's business interests, so now Goldstein is doing the same to Raven.'

'What do you suggest? This isn't exactly a 'return of goods if dissatisfied' kind of business. That said -.'

'No. We're not replacing one batch of drugs with another. I don't want to run the risk of handing him another batch which doesn't get the Goldstein seal of approval. Also, I don't want to get lumbered with the bad drugs. That's the last thing we need.'

'Really? Mr Legitimate Escort Agency. I could line up a buyer in an hour. We split the cash three ways and we all go home happy.'

'How can you possibly be thinking about doing business at a time like this?'

'Drop the sentimentality and grow up. At the end of the day, it's all business. Do you really think that these whores would mourn if you two bozos dropped dead? Of course not. They'd go and fuck for someone else at the drop of a hat. Look at how quickly they moved on from Raven.'

'Raven was a piece of shit who beat the girls and took their money!' retorts Lola with a vigour. Diana doesn't flinch. She won't. Not for anyone.

'I can get us in a room, so to speak, with one of Goldstein's lieutenants. That's not a problem. Just say the word and I'll make a few calls to get us some puro shit. If you're not willing to budge on the drugs thing, what else do you have that Goldstein might want?'

Lola and I look at one another with equal amounts of trepidation and puzzlement. My eyes nervously dance back and forth between Lola and Diana's reflection in the mirror. This goes on for well over a minute with us being no closer to resolving the stalemate once that time has elapsed.

'You mentioned some seed money you had coming your way. How much you got coming down the pike? Enough to make this little situation go away?'

'Well, -.'

'Actually, that's none of your damn business. Besides, that money isn't for us. It's for our girls. It's to give them all the things that we promised them, not to sweep up after your fuck ups. You fucked this up, now you can unfuck it up.'

'I gave you my suggestion and you just wiped your ass with it.'

'Fuck your suggestion! There's got to be something else that you can do. That's what we're paying you for.'

'You're paying me to watch your ass, not wipe it. That's precisely what I'm doing. If I wasn't then you two would be sitting in a jail cell right now on a double murder rap.'

Lola looks right at me. I've been dreading this.

'What is she talking about? Michael? Tell me!'

Closed eyes. Deep breath.

'Oh, you didn't know? Secrets among newlyweds. That's never good. Michael was even kind enough to show me the dissolving bodies. Talk about handing over the smoking gun.'

The cat is now among the pigeons.

'What the fuck Michael?'

'It wasn't like that. I'll explain later on.'

'Explain it to me now.'

Diana honks the horn, driving a welcome stake of respite through the awkward tension. Lola, undeterred, keeps her gaze of daggers fixed on me.

'Guys, what about the trap queen? Nile.'

'How could Nile possibly help us now? Best I can tell he's skipped town.'

'What if we were to find him and give him to Goldstein? Tell Goldstein's men that if he wants Raven then he needs to have a long conversation with Merson. It's a simple exchange, Nile for Honey. We get our girl back, Goldstein gets a lead on Raven, and once Goldstein knows it's us running the girls he'll fuck off until the end of time.'

'Once Goldstein realizes that Merson can't bring him Raven, he's going to kill him!'

Redclay scoffs dismissively and shakes her head. Her cold-blooded demeanour and attitude are more than a little unsettling.

'Either Honey goes or Merson goes.'

'We want no more bloodshed. There can be no more.'

'It ain't floristry! This is how it is. If you want to be in this business, then you have to accept that.'

'There's got to be another way. Besides, he's long gone by now.'

'Well, there is one thing that will bring him back.'

Both exasperated, Lola and I look at one another and sigh, her sigh somewhat muted compared to mine. Neither of us are inclined to ask 'What?', knowing full well that Diana will tell us anyway.

'Do you need me to spell it out for you?'

Again, I don't dare ask her.

'Raven.'

I recline in the seat and close my eyes. By now I've heard enough.

'You've got Raven's burner cells. Drop the boyfriend a text. Tell him things have blown over and you're back in town. We arrange a meet, and when he arrives Goldstein's goons will be there waiting for him.'

This time last week I was en route to Hoover Dam with my best friends in the world, without a care. Now I have the life of someone I barely know in one hand and that of a total stranger in another. Diana sits in silence, texting at a preternatural pace and giving nothing away, while Lola and I quietly ponder the horrifying ultimatum before us.

'I've made the arrangements. Goldstein's man will meet us at Red Rock in an hour. He'll expect an answer. It's all on you now.'

Diana twists the key in the ignition and slowly pulls into the lane to our left. I outstretch my left hand to Lola and almost on cue she slaps the burner cell into my palm. I pass it to my right hand and begin scrolling as we slow down at a red light.

Trawling through Raven's contacts, I land on Nile's name and a lump slowly forms in my throat at the sight of it. One thumb flick later and I'm staring at a blank message beneath his name. I feel like Jack Ruby with my finger on the trigger, leading a man who doesn't know I exist towards certain death.

'HI BAE.'

I hit send and nervously await his response. 'Delivered' gives way to 'Read 11:58' and three wriggling black dots encased in a speech bubble form in the bottom left hand corner of the screen. Each jump of a black circle unseats me further with a heightened sense of dread.

'RAVEN?!?'

'He has no idea.'

CHAPTER 25

Red Rock Canyon. Rustic red rubble on all sides lends the periphery an ethereal charm and beauty. Wiry strings of plants with a silver metallic tint sprout from the soft sand, their shiny sun-aided grey balanced by the few errant green leaves on their paper-thin branches. Hanging like scarecrow arms over the iron vermillion below and shading the many-shaped snaggles of stone that emboss the surface.

The ride here was largely silent, the space between Lola and I growing heavy with the hanging weight of things left unsaid. Difficult conversations waiting to be had on the other side of chaos. Troubling answers festering, congealing in the foreboding heat of dire consequences waiting to combust.

A completely blacked-out Humvee sits ominously opposite our charger in the distance. Diana flashes her lights twice as a signal to the other driver. A pregnant pause ensues and is broken up by an evanescent flicker of the Humvee's headlights. Diana waits a few moments before exiting and placing herself in front of the car. The driver of the Humvee does the same, flanked by two men on each side standing by the doors of the vehicle.

Diana and her opposite number, a tall skinny man in a navy suit and matching fedora stare one another down like two old gunfighters waiting for the other to draw. Nobody moves on either side. Redclay gestures to us with the back of her right hand before taking a bold stride forward. Her counterpart does the same while his colleagues remain stationary, and they eventually meet in the middle.

Lola and I can but look on curiously as this scene unfolds. We can't make out so much as a whisper of their back and forth. The occasional turn of a head on both sides gives nothing away. All hands stay low and from our vantage point the interaction looks less than animated.

'Whatever possessed you to show Redclay the bodies? The whole idea of doing what we did was so that people like her wouldn't find out about Raven and Buford.'

And there it is.

'It wasn't like that at all.'

'Then how was it? The outcome is the same regardless.'

'Remember the beer bottle that showed up in Raven's kitchen while the three of us were at the dollhouse? Redclay was behind that?'

'What are you talking about?'

'While I was minding the house, Redclay showed up. She had a GPS tracker on Raven's car while we were in it. I watched her from the window. She saw the red dirt on the side of the car but she still made a beeline for the house. It was as though she already knew there was something in there and she wanted to make sure it hadn't been moved.'

'That still doesn't explain why you showed her the bodies.'

'I thought I could put a pin in her little leverage game by just being out there with it?'

'Out there?'

'Yes. Feed her a bluff. Show her she couldn't frighten us with blackmail over this.'

'Were you planning to let me in on your brilliant plan?'

Oh boy.

'I'm sorry, OK. I had other things on my mind, like the two bodies in the basement. The two bodies that you put there. And it all happened so fast.'

'If I'd had my way those two carcasses would be below the desert sand by now.'

'Yes, and Diana would have found them, and we'd be none the wiser! Besides, I told her that the biker gang Raven had beef with knew and, along with anyone they had on the inside, they were willing to do anything to protect the people who killed their enemy.'

Normal married couples argue about coffee tables. DIY. What colour to paint the master bedroom. What the hell are we?

'If we're going to talk secrets and not disclosing things then I have a few questions for you Lola.'

'What's that supposed to mean?'

Here it comes.

'Go on!'

Once the bullet is out of the chamber, there's no turning back.

'Alright.'

The hammer is cocked. A sharp intake of breath while I survey the landscape.

'You mentioned before that Jennifer's dad wasn't particularly romantic. Never bought you flowers. But I remember you telling me the morning after our wedding that he took you everywhere. Sounds like two completely different people to me. Which time were you lying, and why did you lie?'

Lola looks apprehensive. Sheepish.

'Michael, please.' Lola's bottom lip quivers as she says this, and she is visibly rattled. 'I'm asking you respectfully, please don't go there.'

My eyes erratically twitch from left to right, mirroring a mind caught between two instincts which it knows to both be right but for very different reasons. I turn and face the front, leaving the nervous stand-off to dissolve in the sullen silence.

For the first time I see Lola's impervious walls come down fully as she quietly sheds a little tear. The blood drops from her face as she lightly sniffles and a second tear runs into the first, punctuated by a yelping whimper. Lola's expression collapses under the might of her affected composure from the last few days.

I lean over and throw my arms around Lola before tenderly bringing her head in towards my chest. Lola's palms gently rub my arms as I softly kiss her on the dome while rubbing the back of her head with my right hand.

'It's alright. I've got you, Lola. I've got you. Whatever you have to face, you no longer have to face it alone. We're one now. I mean it.'

'You're a great man, Michael. You know that?'

Lola nestles her head further into my chest, pressing her right cheek against my heart. She rubs the side of her face against my torso and firmly squeezes my arms.

'I'm trying to be. For you. For us. Listen, whatever you have to tell me, you tell me when you're good and ready. I'm here for you. Always.'

'Thank you.'

Lola's mood settles in the silence that follows. She roughly dries her eyes with the ball of her left palm. Lola has shown me a broken wing, and is all the more beautiful for it. Something terrible happened to my wife, exactly what I don't know, but she survived and she is strong.

'You're a warrior.'

She lets out a sweet little laugh. Part modesty, part surprise.

'I mean it. You've held everything together these last few days. I saw how strong you were in the face of everything that happened. You're iron.'

Her eyes now dry, Lola tilts her head upwards and looks right at me. I love this woman and I always will.

The driver's side door suddenly clicks open and shut as Diana slides back into the car.

'Let's go. We'll lead, they'll follow.'

Diana sticks the key in and starts the engine. With one hand on the steering wheel, she turns her head and looks back at the two of us.

'If anyone asks, you hacked Raven's phone and cloned his number.'

Lola and I look at one another, confused.

'While you two were pouting earlier on, I was thinking.'

CHAPTER 26

I sit opposite Lola at a long and crowded table, all of the seats occupied except for those directly either side of us. My gaze lingers over Lola's right shoulder and through the floor-to-ceiling window behind her towards the entrance of Tommy Hilfiger. It's the top of the hour and there's still no sign of Nile.

Growing more restless by the minute, I take a bite out of my Philly cheesesteak before looking up and out again.

'Where the devil is he?'

'Try texting him again. The traffic has been pretty bad all day.'

'Is there any way he suspects that it's a trap?'

It's a fair question, all things considered.

'How the fuck should I know?'

It's good to see Lola's spirits back up after earlier.

'You've definitely perked up.'

'If Nile doesn't bring his lousy self here, we've got nothing.'

'And Goldstein still has Honey.'

'You're new to this town and don't know about Goldstein's reputation, but trust me, we do not want to have to go to him and tell him that this has all been a huge waste of time.'

'You're not exactly a Vegas veteran yourself, Miss Pittsburgh.'

'Folk can smell the jumbo jet off you a mile away!'

Ha. She's got me there.

'The girls talk. A lot. I've heard enough stories to know that Goldstein is not to be crossed.'

We're in one of them right now.

'Let me guess, he once trapped someone's head in a vice because they burnt his toast?'

Lola scoffs lightly and shakes her head.

'We're already deceiving him' I say. 'So, I guess we've already crossed him.'

'Only if he finds out.'

I take another bite out of my cheesesteak and a sip of cola before pulling the burner phone out with my right hand. After a quick scroll I land on the earlier text trail with Nile and begin pounding the buttons furiously with my thumb.

'WHERE THE FUCK ARE YOU? EVER HEAR OF BEING ON TIME?'

Message sent. Message delivered. I stare at the screen waiting for the words and numbers to give way to a read acknowledgement. The seconds linger and each fresh, nervous blink renews that dreaded view.

The black lettering on the screen begins to twitch from side to side under my apprehensive gaze. I hear a piercing ring in my head which silences everything else in my view as my shaky vision slips into a fuzzy blur. A distant whisper materializes all of a sudden, saying something over and over which I can't fully make out.

'Michael!'

'Huh?!'

Lola startles me when she slides her right across the table and gently clutches my right bicep. My train of thought has completely drifted off and I need a moment to get my bearings.

'I think we better call Nile. Now.'

'Will you excuse me for a moment.'

'But…. .'

I stand up and walk away from the table, turning left and heading for the men's room. My head feels heavy yet numb at the same time as I walk past the growing throng of people lining up with trays by the kitchen.

Upon reaching the bathroom door, I extend my left arm towards the wall beside me and meekly bow my head. Between deep breaths horrible thoughts of Honey coming to severe physical harm and even death fill my mind. Nausea sets in and I feel like I'm going to throw up or cry right here and now.

'Oh God.'

I squeeze my eyes shut tighter and let out a tense gasp of air before lifting my head back up. Upon re-opening my eyes, I feel my head and whole body quickly settle. Pushing myself back off the adjacent wall, I reach for the bathroom door handle with my right hand and let myself in.

After closing the door behind me I'm greeted by the sight of a man bending down and snorting a line of cocaine off the sink area through a short plastic implement. He quickly stands up and jerks his head back, letting out a mild growl as he does so. Stopped in my tracks, I methodically scan his weary face as he looks in the mirror.

It's Nile.

I click the door locked behind me without looking while keeping my sights locked on the reflection in the mirror. My chest lightly shakes in the face of the sudden terror and the thought of what's about to happen. I don't like it but it has to go down like this. There is no other way.

My phone is back at the table. It's just Nile and myself. No Lola, no Diana, none of Goldstein's goons. Just us. I kneel down and reach for the laces on my right shoe with both hands, never taking my eyes off Nile as he prepares another bump. He doesn't appear to notice me.

Flicking my gaze between Nile and my shoe, I strategically place my left hand in front of my right and covertly use the latter to pull out a long shoelace. I grab the other end in my left and slowly rise to my feet, clutching the makeshift weapon below my waist. As Nile examines the short line of white powder I begin the short walk across, eyeing the spot directly behind him.

Nile bends over to take a snort as I settle into his blind spot. Seizing the opportunity, I throw the shoelace over his head and pull back on his throat, yanking Nile back into an upright position while pressing my right knee into the small of his back.

He gurgles and grunts, feebly trying to reach for the lace with his right hand while curling his left hand behind his back towards something tucked under the tail of his shirt. I drive my right knee further into the base of his spine, pushing his stomach right up against the edge of the sink area. His left arm freezes by his side while he swings and misses with wild elbows using his right.

A sharp, stinging pang from the heel of Nile's left boot hits the middle of my left shin, causing me to fall and relinquish my grip on the shoelace before doubling over in pain. He nails me while I'm on the ground with a swift kick to the stomach. The blow hits my gut like a swinging brick and leaves me winded on my back.

Nile reaches into the back of his waistband with his left hand and draws a knife before lunging downwards to me with both hands clasped around the weapon. Riding on pure adrenaline and instinct, I sit up and grab his wrists. The blade shakes whilst moving neither forwards nor backwards. My heart pumping ever faster, I manage to roll Nile onto his back. His grip on the blade doesn't relinquish.

Tiny miscreant beads of sweat run down my face and into my eyes while we exchange pained grimaces. I manage to twist Nile's grip and the blade slightly to the left and away from my torso before instinctively spitting in Nile's eye. He flinches, his grunting giving way to a guttural yawp before I push the knife out of his now tenuous grip and kick it along the floor to my left.

My knee in his stomach and hands around his neck, I nail Nile with a thrusting headbutt which drives his head into the floor beneath. His eyelids droop down over his big brown eyes as his head rolls in slow motion to his left.

'My goodness.'

CHAPTER 27

It's a lot of miles back towards home, each one made longer and colder and harsher by what's now in our rear view. Honey is sprawled across the backseats, sound asleep and blissfully unaware of what it took to get her back. I stare into the darkness straight ahead, my eyeballs weighing heavy with the gravity of the night's events. The view before me is but a blur of pitch black specked with flashes of zipping light from the passing cars on all sides.

Barely a word has passed between Lola and I since we got in the car to head for home. My gaze doesn't twitch in either direction and my thoughts don't wander far from the haunting shadow of Nile's face in that fateful moment. Every few seconds my mind slips off into a train of mindless rubbish, but stark reality has it on a short leash and yanks hard every single time.

Is this all that this life is? Bloodshed, cheating death, stealing solace, bartering lives we deem less valuable in return for others which we can commercialize. Do we pick up the pieces and retreat from the debris field just so that we can survive enough to make it to the next, each one bearing a choice of meeting our end or continuing on through a world of even more hurt?

The tinned walls on all sides of the shipping container are dull, dank and falling apart with rust. Nondescript boxes line the perimeter, adding to the daunting coldness of the clinical interior. Rectangles of florescent light up above barely breach the grainy all-encompassing grey with a slither of errant white.

Lola and I stand behind and either side of Harley, Goldstein's middleman, forming a triangle before a shrouded figure bound to a wooden chair by silver duct tape wrapped around his torso. Further tape binds his wrists together behind his back, rendering him completely immobile. After several seconds Harley steps forward and abruptly removes the shroud with his right hand, revealing Nile's sweaty, dishevelled face and eyes filled with terror.

Nile, mouth gaping open, lets out a tentative sigh and slowly rolls his head over his right shoulder before locking his eyes on me hard. He glares at me through a frazzled glaze while his mouth feebly attempts to curl up into a scowl.

'Hey, I remember you' Nile declares through a hoarse croak. 'You're the guy who jumped me in the bathroom. What the fuck do you want?'

Harley leans in towards Nile and snaps the fingers on his right hand in front of his face. Nile's bleary eyes shift away from me and now focus on Harley.

'You know damn well what we want. Your boyfriend, Raven. Where is he?'

Nile, clearly petrified, looks up at Harley with an expression of pleading contrition.

'I don't know where he is. I swear. Haven't seen or heard from him since Sunday.'

'That's too bad. My boss is out $3 million thanks to your Dipshit Romeo. You tell us where he is, he comes down here to straighten things out and you're free to go.'

Nile doesn't respond.

'No? So if I call Raven right now and tell him you're here with me, he won't get his ass down here faster than a jackrabbit to save your lousy behind? I guess he's not that into you after all. What he is into, however, is my boss for three mill'. At this point he's willing to accept drugs or cash. Failing that, we'll just take it out of your ass, right here, right now.'

Harley arches back upright before taking two ominous steps backwards and drawing a silver gun with his right hand. Holding the gun sideways, he slicks the hammer back with his thumb and lowers his aim square towards Nile's chest.

'I'm going to count to three. There will not be a four.'

He can count to a million, it won't bring him any closer to Raven. I've boxed Nile in and left him facing a grisly end that he can't outrun, no matter what he does. The dice are loaded and he has absolutely no idea. Neither does Harley. I don't like it but it has to happen this way. Either he's on the receiving end of that bullet or Honey is.

'Look, Nile' interjects Lola, convincingly maintaining the subterfuge. 'Just tell him where Raven is and this will all be over. We can all go home.'

'I already told you. I don't know.'

Nile is shaking, his lips quivering and teeth lightly chattering. He looks at Lola imploringly, but her expression doesn't budge. All we can do now is try to stall Harley for as long as possible. My turn now.

'That's a lot of loyalty to a scumbag who'd sell you down the river to save himself. You think he loves you? If he did, he wouldn't let you take the fall for his fuck up. See how he skipped town without coming to get you first?'

'I know he loves me. He laid low for a couple of days until the heat died down a little. Then he came back to get me. We were going to meet at the outlet mall today and get out of town together. It was all going fine until this fucking bozo jumped me.'

Harley pops off a quick warning shot which claps against the ceiling, the metal on metal collision making a rapid snapping sound.

'Enough foreplay!'

Silence. That one shot sucked the air right out of the room. There's no way now to halt the horrible certainty.

'You've got one last chance, Trap Queen. Tell me where Raven is, or you're going bye-bye.'

'I don't know where he is! How many times do I have to tell you?'

The power of a lie. It can knot a noose on all sides for some, while setting others free.'

'One.'

Nile is a bad man who chose to live in a dangerous world. This was bound to happen, if not at our hands, then someone else's. All we did was hasten the axe that loomed long in the shadows.

'Two.'

Are we any different from or better than Nile for the choice that we made? His demise isn't about him choosing to live in a dangerous world, but rather us choosing to survive in it and preserve what's ours. It's been said that the only justification for taking a life is to save another, but are we all that noble when our consideration for the life we're saving is purely financial?

'Three.'

Harley raises the gun so that the barrel is pointed squarely at Nile's head. Nile, knowing what's coming, quietly winces and closes his eyes.

'Wait! Wait! Wait!' I yell at Harley, prompting him to turn his head to the left and look at me. His grip on the gun and his aim don't shift an inch. 'You don't need to do this.'

'Give me one good reason why the hell not.'

'Raven's gone. Nobody knows where to or how long for. What we do know, however, is that his Treasure Island vice business is ours. We bought him out on Monday. What if, instead of buying the patch from

Raven, we buy it from your boss? He takes Treasure Island in lieu of what he's owed and we pay back the debt over the course of a year. Monthly payments. No vig. If we miss one then we lose the patch right back to Goldstein.'

'Are you for real?' Lola is incredulous. 'Are you really suggesting that we pay $3 million for something that we already bought for fifty grand, just to save this little shitbird's life? Are you out of your fucking mind?'

It would be understandable, given the circumstances. I ignore Lola and keep my focus on Harley.

'Look, Harley, we can get you the first million in cash first thing Monday morning. No word of a lie.'

Toupee Shakur, you've done me a kindness.

'You know it makes sense, Harley. At the end of the day, we're in business to make money. You don't have to kill Nile. We're good for every single penny.'

Harley lowers the gun back by his waist and turns his whole body towards me.

'$1 million down on Monday morning, and then a hundred and sixty five grand a month for a year?'

'That's exactly right.'

He walks across to me and stands right in front, eyeballing me but saying nothing. I hear the hammer of his gun softly click forward while his eyes remain locked on mine.

'You sure can talk a good game.'

Don't sell it. He is right, though. Last I checked, just a few hours ago, the three million I stole through Raj was still running through that maze of offshore accounts. It's not home and dry yet. By 5 P.M. tomorrow we should have it right where we want it.

'You better not screw up with the first million. You'll lose a lot more than your patch if you do.'

Show him nothing. Tell him even less.

'And by the way, you open up shop a week from Monday.'

Shit.

'I'll give you a call with the details for the drop. I'm only going to tell you once. Don't even think about being late.'

Harley pulls out a phone in his left hand and quickly sends a text before looking back at me.

'Honey is free to go.'

At last.

'She'll meet you by your car in fifteen.'

'Great. I trust that she hasn't been harmed.'

'Of course not. She's been holed up in Goldstein's penthouse this whole time. As far as she's concerned, she got picked up by a really great client and lost her phone, which will be miraculously returned to her right about now. And yes, the meter has been running from minute one. Honey caught herself a real gravy train here. No sex, lots of conversation, champagne, luxury.'

'Bullshit.'

'No bullshit. Honey's innocent in all this. We weren't going to harm her unless we absolutely had to. She was just a bargaining chip. I wish we could have found Waterboy here in the first place, but he was nowhere to be found.'

Each passing word feels like another spike on the road to all this being over, heightening my sense of anxiety as the seconds fall off the clock.

'Speaking of which…. .'

Harley extends his right hand to me with the gun in it, the handle pointing out towards me. Confused and perturbed, I look at Harley and then down at the gun before glancing back up towards Harley.

'What is this?'

He looks right at me with eyes like daggers. It's as though he expects me to know what he's thinking right now.

'You were right.'

'What?'

'You've agreed to clear Raven's debt, so now there's no need for me to kill Nile.'

OK.

'Which is why you're going to do it.'

What?

'What?'

'You heard me.'

'This is fucking nuts!' Lola's right. This makes no sense. Harley briefly turns his head back to look at Lola before glancing back at me.

'I don't need him to bring me Raven and the money, so I've got no use for him now.'

Wow.

'Unless you were planning to offer him a job, ha ha.'

'Look, I'll do anything you want. Please. I just don't want to die.'

'YOU SHUT UP!'

Harley's roar truly stuns me. He's stood once again facing Nile, the gun pointed squarely at his head.

'Harley, he's right. There's got to be another way.'

He slowly turns back towards me, head first and then the rest of his body, before offering me the gun again.

'Goldstein's going to get his money. Why are you doing this?'

Harley quietly smirks and shakes his head.

'The money's taken care of. This is about respect.'

'Respect?'

'Yes.'

I don't follow. The best thing to do is just nod and agree.

'You two are springing for Raven's debt, meaning Raven never paid up. What kind of message would Goldstein be sending if someone screwed him out of three million, didn't pay up and lived to tell the tale?'

So, I've just indebted us to Vegas's deadliest mobster for nothing?

'Either Raven goes, or Nile goes, and I don't see Raven here.'

He's determined to make a body, any body, turn cold.

'And why me? Why do I have to do it?'

'Like you said, I don't have to.'

Fucker.

'The sooner you do this, the sooner you can get home and take Honey with you.'

He takes my right hand in his left and firmly presses the fun into my palm. My eyes nervously dance back and forth between the weapon and Harley's unflinching expression.

'I'm going to make it easy for you. It's either him or Honey.'

I flick him an imploring look, but he doesn't bite. Harley takes two steps to his right, turns around and facetiously sweeps his right arm low from left to right, signalling.

'Shit.'

After a few moments of hesitation, I tentatively wrap my sweaty palm around the gun and drop it by my side. I look over at Nile and he looks back at me sheepishly. He doesn't know it, but I'm every bit as scared as he is.

'I'm sorry' I mouth, almost tearful.

One look down at the gun and then another back up at Nile. I don't want this, but this is how it has to be.

'Alright.'

Looking over, I catch Lola's solemn nod of reassurance and acknowledge it with one of my own. For a moment I close my eyes and steal a deep breath before focusing again on Nile.

One foot directly in front of the other, pacing forward, just like we did when we were kids to measure ten yards before a free kick. My heart weighs heavier with each step and my stomach stirs hard. As I make the long short walk Nile is but a blurred speck in the corner of my left eye, while my right hand meekly tremors by my hip. The Claddagh ring on my finger taps against the gun, ringing out a chilling click of metal on metal that punctures the quiet chill in the air.

Standing level with Nile, I stop short in my tracks and stare at my feet. Lifting my head up to look straight ahead, the gravity of what I'm about to do hits home hard. It was one thing laying the trap to get him to his final resting place, but being his executioner is quite another. Bound certainly by the whip hand of a chilling ultimatum, but shackled just as much by a choice I made almost a week ago. A choice that ultimately brought me here.

I am a reluctant hangman under the gun of my own misguided folly. But a hangman all the same.

Do it fast and then let it go. It'll be like turning off a light.

'I'm sorry.'

ONE!

TWO!

THREE!

FOUR!

FIVE!

Tears run down my face at the sounding of the final shot. My cold breath, leaden with fear and horror, meshes with the thick cloud of hot gun smoke as I look upon Nile's lifeless body. Crimson seeping from the closely connected wounds in his chest, head tilted back. Mouth agape yet inanimate and eyes dulled where just moments ago there was light.

Who am I?

It's a lot of miles back to normality after what I did tonight.

But I've spent years running from normal.

And I'm not going back.

CHAPTER 28

The morning after the murder before. I guess at this point I was supposed to feel something different. Haunted and afflicted by the horror of what I'm capable of, what I have been capable of all along. What's truly frightening is that other than the initial whirlwind of tumult on the way home, I've felt nothing like that. No guilt. Nothing.

I suddenly feel strangely unburdened, like I've somehow shed shrink wrap that was coming between myself and the person I want and need to be. What's the difference between the two? Is it that one is a burgeoning mass of thoughts and impulses, while the other is what happens when those inclinations become actions?

Lola, a beautiful stranger just a week ago, is now my rock. Because of her I now see and believe that so much more than I knew before is possible. She simply radiates strength, and her iron will is somewhat infectious, unnervingly so at times. I admire her. I respect her. I do truly love her above everything else, as crazy as it might sound given the brevity of our relationship. She's a true force of nature.

Ten days now including today before we open up shop. It's been imposed upon us but we have to make the best of it now. When you've been given a choice which isn't really a choice, you take that choice. The consequences of the alternative aren't worth thinking about.

Jennifer is at pre-school, so it's just Lola and I at home. The sweet warmth of her delicious black coffee charms my insides. Sitting comfortably on the black leather sofa in our living room, the laptop screen before us delivers good news. My $3 million severance package, minus 7.5% in stoppages, has arrived at its final destination. $2,775,000. The wheels are turning now, and Top Drawer Entertainment is now open for business.

'One week from Monday is opening day' says Lola, emphatic as always. 'And already we're short-handed. Our business model is no good now. Ten girls and a $600,000 monthly revenue stream won't cut it. Half of that cash is earmarked for commission, and then Goldstein's loan repayment cuts what's left by more than half.'

'May I remind you that there are 16 girls holed up in that house?'

'Eight of whom we can't use because they're fucking cokeheads! However you slice it, we need a lot more than what we've got right now to cover our indirect costs and make good on the margins we talked about before.

'I don't see what the problem is. They'll be making enough money to get rehabbed in their own time.'

'Tell me you did not just say that!'

I'm not about to start lying to my new wife. Again.

'We don't pimp out addicts. We're not Raven. Remember what we promised before? 150 grand for anyone we have to future endeavour.'

'That was before a million got swallowed up by Goldstein. Maybe we should park your lofty ideals until we're making money.'

'We're down a million because of a deal that you made. To what? To spare some degenerate you ended up killing anyway.'

She's got me there.

'The lofty ideals as you call them stay!'

That iron will in full effect.

'Alright. Alright. Goldstein leaves us out a full million, there's nothing we can do about that. We're now left with 1.775.'

'150 large each for eight girls. That's another 1.2 gone.'

'25 grand apiece for the remainers, plus their guarantee for the week. There goes 208 on top of the 1.2.'

'Plus, we need to recruit more girls. Eight to be exact.'

'Double that figure of 208. 416. Now there's 159 left in the pot.'

'We help the girls like we said. Get them fixed up with new apartments and all that.'

'Then there's the website for the agency and our office space. I suggest a room at Treasure Island that we pay for by the week.'

'OK. We're also going to need administrative support to falsify bookings, clean the money trail and otherwise maintain the illusion of a legitimate escort agency.'

'We can get in a couple of college kids from UNLV and slip them each a C-note a day.' Lola nods in approval and smiles.

'Next week I'm gonna start up the paperwork to get the girls their benefits.'

'Great. Do it. We also need to think about a second location.' Lola nods again.

'Now there's the small matter of recruiting. We need to bring in eight girls and have them ready to work the week after next. Where do we start? This being Vegas, there's no shortage of options. But we need to make sure that we get the right girls.'

'I'm one step ahead of you there.'

'Do tell.'

Drumroll please.

'I exchanged details with the strippers from my bachelor party, all four of them. Thought they might be worth recruiting further down the line. Two of them in particular, Gabriella and Candy, have a lot of earning potential.'

'Doing business at your bachelor party? I'm impressed.'

Lola's words bring a modest smile to my face.

'What about the other four?'

'We hit Sapphires this weekend. Just before I met you, I spent a night in there.'

'I remember. You were buzzing. So, who was it that got you all revved up?'

'Ariella, Lolly, Kiana and Jay.'

'Wow. I'm glad you had to stop and think about it.'

'All four of them are real thoroughbreds.'

'Thoroughbreds?' Lola shoots me a puzzled look.

'Er, yeah. I heard that in *The Sopranos*.'

Lola shakes her head and lets out a light chuckle.

'Anyway, I know none of them are working for anyone else right now.'

'How do you know?'

This is going to be a little awkward.

'I, er, I asked.'

'You asked, just like that?'

'The driver who took us to the club told us that a lot of the girls in there offer 'additional services', as he called them.'

This next part should be fun.

'Additional services?'

'Yeah.'

She looks at me, waiting for me to say something. Anything.

'Er…. .'

I was wrong. This part isn't fun at all.

'Well, Paresh, my roommate, and I were talking about getting some room service the next day. So, we thought we'd ask around.'

'I'm sorry, room service?'

'Yeah.'

Uh-oh.

'So that morning when I met you at the bar, it wasn't pure chance? You were actively looking for room service, as you call it. Didn't matter whose it was, you were just happy to take whatever was going.'

Least said, soonest mended.

'If I'm not mistaken, it could be one of those Sapphires bimbos sitting here with you planning an empire instead of me. It just so happened that they weren't selling what you were buying, but I was.'

Fuck. Cue the inevitable awkward silence. One potato, two potato, three potato.... .'

'I'm totally fucking with you!'

Lola and I share a hearty, raucous laugh when it's all said and done. When she laughs her whole face lights up and her rapturous zeal is contagious.

'Your face, Michael! Your face!'

CHAPTER 29

Sapphires. Back where it all began. Not exactly regular Saturday night date night fare, but what the hell? Lola and I stand in front of the crowded bar sipping Bucklers from long-necked bottles while bathing in the hard blue light.

A pretty young Indian lady with Earthen brown skin and bobbed hair as black and silkily shiny as vinyl works the stage in front of us. She slides her perfect near-naked form split-legged down a pole towards a mirrored surface laden with dollar bills of various denominations, an endlessly replenishing pile.

'What time are we meeting your bachelor party girls on Monday? And tell me their names again.'

'One o'clock at Victoria's Secret. We're going to be meeting Candy, Gabriella, Kelly & Pantera.'

'Pantera? Interesting.'

'As fate would have it, I know Pantera's cousin from the London poetry circuit.'

'Really? No way.'

'Oh yes. Lin Manuel. He's an amazing poet, singer, and guitarist from Gibraltar. We co-headlined a Valentine's Day poetry event in London a few years ago.'

'Nice.'

'It was a great night. First time I ever got paid for my poetry. Made the princely sum of £10.'

Lola chuckles at this with a smile.

'Is she British?'

'Yes, she is. By way of Mauritius, India, Ireland, and Italy.'

'Oh wow!'

'She's quite something.'

'Sounds like it.'

I take another sip of beer while the crowd around the stage grows louder and more rambunctious. A vivacious blonde in a tight black dress makes her way over from the left and stops right in front of me.

'Hi there.'

Her accent is a sweet Slavic tome of indeterminate precise origin. Charming. Almost musical.

'You wanna go private?'

Talk about cutting right to the chase.

'What's Your name?'

'My name is You Wanna Go Private?'

She's eager. I'm not sure if I like it.

'Maybe later.'

'OK.'

The blonde walks away, poorly masking her disappointment with a weak smile. I take another swig of beer and turn to Lola on my right.

'Tell me Lola, what would you say to the Flamingo as our second location? We have eight players on each patch and we switch them over every few nights.'

'Sounds good to me. It's a great spot. A lot of history with Bugsy Siegel and all that.'

'Indeed. Very appropriate, all things considered.'

'Maybe one day people will talk about the two of us and our exploits there.'

'Wouldn't that be something.'

We clink bottles and we're all smiles. Something that was unfathomable just a couple of weeks ago is now a reality. The shadow of Goldstein and the stark fact of what that could become, along with the dark memory of what I did to get us here, sporadically breezes in to menacingly bend the palm trees in this new paradise. Yet strangely I feel more at peace keeping those things at bay than I ever did trying to hold back the waning hours on a Sunday night ahead of another week of office humdrum.

'One more thing' states Lola. 'Seeing as we now have a larger operation on our hands, we should think about delegating more.'

She had me at 'One more thing.' She always has me.

'What do you have in mind?'

'We appoint two team leaders to run the shifts. Give them an extra $500 each per week and the rest of the girls report to them. They make the schedule, handle the concerns from the other girls and report into us.'

'That's a great idea.'

'I'll choose one team leader and you choose the other.'

'You're on.'

'I kinda see a lot of myself in Honey. She's steely, resilient. There's a certain fire in her eyes.'

'Good call. I definitely know what you mean. The way she stood up to Redclay, you've got to respect that.'

'How about you? Who's your pick.'

'I think Pantera would be a great fit, assuming that she accepts our offer.'

'Why wouldn't she?'

I nod in agreement through a swigged mouthful of beer, the bottle pressed firmly against my lips.

'Of the trio from the bus, she's definitely the loudest and most vibrant. You can tell that she's the de facto leader of the group.'

'I trust your judgement.'

And I'm sure of my own instincts in a way that I never have been before outside of the classroom.

'Let's get this done nice and quick. We might even be able to catch Tiesto at Hakassan before we go home.'

Lola smiles and takes another sip of beer before responding.

'We should rest up tomorrow. Take Jennifer to the park. We've got an early start on Monday with the drop-off.'

'You're right. Park it is.'

'So, who's first on the list for tonight?'

'That would be Ariella.'

'You see her?'

'Not yet.'

'Keep looking. I'll grab us two more beers.'

Lola walks away, looking around and trying to join the disjointed queue at the bar which has no clear beginning or end. I take one last sip of beer and look for somewhere to leave the drained bottle before feeling a gentle dainty hand against the base of my back.

'Hey you. I thought I saw you from the floor.'

She walks in front and turns to face me. A familiar face from the small hours of Friday morning. Her silky brown hair is up in a neat hive and she's wearing a figure-hugging sky blue dress which accentuates her large breasts and smooth skin. Her doll-like facial features and olive-porcelain complexion imbues her mixture of Japanese and Hawaiian ancestry.

'Kiana.'

'How you doing?'

'All the better for having seen you.'

'Oh stop it.'

I mean it. This is what we came for. Tonight is all business.

'You looking for anything special tonight?'

'Actually I am.'

Kiana tilts her head to the right in anticipation of what I'm going to say next.

'I'm here with my wife tonight.'

'Your wife?'

'Yes. It's amazing what can happen in one week.'

'Wow.'

'I guess you could call this date night.'

Kiana bows her head and laughs quietly. It's sweet and endearing.

'My wife's at the bar. Why don't you grab Ariella, and we can all head to the VIP for a little tag team action.'

'Wow. You're really going all in tonight.'

'You bet.'

All in and for the first time ever I'm betting entirely on myself, expecting rather than merely hoping for the amazing.

CHAPTER 30

Opening night. Treasure Island is abuzz with the usual throng of human traffic and pealing of computerised bells on all sides. Lola and I sit at the head of the bar sipping O'Doul's, looking like anybody else on the floor while hiding in plain sight as the criminal power brokers that we truly are.

We're watching every inch, we're calling all the plays. Nothing here moves without our say-so. After a couple of hours, we will head to the Flamingo and run the same backseat driving routine before retiring for the evening. Give it a month, maybe two, and we'll cut the apron strings, leaving the girls to their own devices.

On the left sit Pantera and Gabriella, and on the right Jay and Lolly. They line up at the opposite end of the bar with two empty seats separating them. Each pair of girls separated by two empty seats and each one having a unique empty seat either side of them. Their designer purses rest on the surface of the bar next to their clear non-alcoholic beverages in plastic cups. To the casual onlooker there's nothing out of the ordinary going on, but in reality everything happening right here and now is very much tactical.

Mona and Suzy, neither of them really playing the machines in front of them, wait in the wings on the left, while Sylvia and Davina do the same on the right. Each one of them is watching the backs of the girls at the bar and waiting to step up as soon as one of them departs with a client. They know their running order and they know what to do.

The quartet at the bar wait for codewords and signals from the girls behind them. These cues will tell them when there is a potential John incoming and also when to move seats to greet a gentleman further down the bar. We second these cues from our vantage point in case they are missed.

We care deeply about the safety of our girls, therefore we have one signal that matters more than any other. If someone is lurking who looks like trouble, too inebriated, too aggressive or whatever, my pen goes up and purses go on seats. We've already had that once tonight. A sloppy drunk who came staggering out of the Chinese restaurant, espousing 9/11 conspiracy theories and ranting about 'That Cuban bitch.'

Not much footfall at the bar so far, but the night is young. We've built it, so they will come. Those who come not knowing it's built, just like myself on that fateful Friday morning, will be reeled in good and hard. Several groups from the real estate conference at this hotel are currently dining and drinking at the American-Chinese hybrid restaurant in the foreground, many of the sharp-suited men in ebullient form as the alcohol flows freely.

They're eyeing up the merchandise, and we're watching them and everything else like two all-seeing pit bosses. The girls follow our covert instructions and don't look over towards the diners. These men like what they see, so much so that they don't even notice Lola and I tracing their admiring looks with our eyes.

All of the girls at the bar draw leering looks. Particularly popular are Gabriella, the vivacious and voluptuous Brazilian brunette whose curves conjure memories of Jayne Mansfield, and Lolly, a pretty and petite Afro-Cuban with short black hair and a form-fitting navy dress. If the new girls are at all nervous it certainly does not show.

The two Filipino bartenders, Robert and Cristobal, are an absolute class act. I will slip them both a C-note for their trouble before we leave. I politely signal to Cristobal to come over using two fingers of my right hand and he duly approaches with a big smile on his face.

'We'll take another round. Keep the tab open. And send two bottles of Dom Perignon to that front table in the restaurant. If they ask, tell them it's on the house.'

'Right away Sir.'

'Thank you.'

Cristobal retreats to the bar and whispers something to Robert while gently pointing our way.

'What was that?' asks Lola with a hint of a laugh in her voice.

'It's a push. You'll see.'

'OK.'

'Their last two rounds have all been dark liquor. They're all one glass away from being morose. Gotta get 'em pepped up again and spending their money over here before they start crying over the deals they didn't quite close today.'

'Wow. You really have been paying attention to them.'

'Of course.'

Robert comes over and lays a cool bottle of O'Doul's and a fresh Treasure Island napkin before each of us.

'Gracias Robert.'

'De nada.'

Lola looks at me with an impressed smile.

'Look at you with that Espanol! Muy bien!'

I tip my bottle towards Lola before taking a sip. As the cooling nectar drenches my dry mouth, Cristobal leaves the restaurant table and begins to slowly make his way back towards us. I look down at my phone and go through the messages in the Flamingo group chat.

Everyone is present and correct, checked in and keeping score of their evening's activity:

- Honey - 1
- Kelly - 1
- Kiana - 1
- Ariella - 0
- Candy - 1
- Caprice - 0
- Emily - 0
- Michelle - 0

The night is young and half the team there are already off the mark, while over here business is about to pick up.

'Sir, the gentlemen asked for four more glasses plus the four girls at the bar.'

'If those girls are happy to join them then why not?'

Blondie's *Heart of Glass* begins to play while Cristobal quietly confers with Lolly and Jay. After he stops talking the girls look over to us. I give them a subtle nod of approval and almost on cue they disembark, making their way around the bar towards the other side. Cristobal and I repeat this routine with Gabriella and Pantera as Lola signals to the girls on the flanks to slowly approach the bar.

The flirtatious foursome buoyantly sashay towards the front table and perch themselves on the laps of jolly partying realtors as their seats at the bar get filled. Cristobal enters behind them with four skinny champagne flutes in a silver ice bucket. Robert begins clearing away the near-empty plastic cups and taking drinks orders from the reinforcements.

Self-satisfied laughs erupt from the table while glasses quickly fill up with champagne. The party is in full swing and showing no signs of waning. Successive pings emanate from my phone. I don't look but the activity brings a smile to my face.

In the foreground a bleary-eyed man with his tie crooked around his neck stands up from the table and points towards the bar. There's a slight stumble in his step but at the same time he's showing no signs of slowing down his wild night of partying. Here for a good time, not a long time.

'I'll take a round of those four if there's one going!'

I give the girls the signal. They know what to do.

CHAPTER 31

I love this time of year. A sense of giddy childlike excitement sets in as my heart wells up with anticipation for what's coming. That one day of commencement and celebration that follows a charming season of advent calendar days where the celebratory spirit clings unrelentingly to the atmosphere.

Christmas.

Every year this serves as a time for reflection. To look back at the year that was and also to look ahead, resolve. So many times I've found myself winding down the same year as the last. This would always be followed by a plan for a new tomorrow that would never come. New job, girlfriend. This time it will happen, I said every single time.

29 has been different in ways I could never have imagined. I took control of my destiny, found gears in myself which I didn't know existed. Layers of my soul which for so long laid buried and silent beneath the dust from the churn of the nine to five hamster wheel.

And, of course, there's Lola.

As the holiday progressed, I began to have my *Shirley Valentine* moment. Slowly discovering another side of myself, but not really knowing what it was. I could feel it the previous Saturday morning during the 17-Mile Drive, standing atop that mountain and looking out into the distance. Beyond the beautiful Monterey vista lay a future completely unlike the past.

Lola turned on a light inside me and I saw what that future was. I've felt that holiday euphoria before. Barcelona in July of last year. Amsterdam in February. That sensation of being in a place where nobody knows me. Where I can be somebody else, even for just a couple of days. But I was always just me again once it was all over.

This trip was different. That bored little boy from before was now a man truly lost. I'd started to question all that I was and everything I'd ever done. Could I change? Should I make myself different, even if it means betraying every inclination that I have, all of the impulses and idiosyncrasies that make me, well, me? How I longed to fall off the same assembly line as everyone else, simply because, in my mind at least, it meant no longer being lonely.

Ironically, given my past malaise, I found freedom not in conforming but in further blazing my own trail. Lighting those flames brighter and harder than ever before and contorting them in a dangerous new direction which only I can follow. Nagging voices whispering all the other ways the Nile situation could have gone down occasionally rear their head, but the anti-anxiety meds usually silence them.

November was a very satisfying month. Lola and I stand before the double bed in the Treasure Island hotel room which serves as our office, staring at a neat pile of $100 bills arranged into neat stacks of $10,000 each.

'$768,000. That's an outstanding first month.' I nod my head in agreement with Lola's statement before folding my arms.

'Outstanding it is Lola. Outstanding it is.'

Lola looks at me and smiles.

'384 needs to come out for commission, leaving us with another 384.' My wife is all business, the gears in her head turning hard behind her Earthen eyes as I crunch the numbers. 'Next, we've got salaries. Fifteen for our two team leaders. Seventy for the rest of the team, fifty for the two of us. So, 249 after payroll.'

Lola's expression is flat and neutral.

'249 after salaries and commission' she replies.

'Yes.'

'Then there's benefits. Fifty-two for pensions and eighteen for health insurance. On top of that there's a grand for Alton and Emmanuel.'

'178.'

'Four grand for us to work out of here for the month.'

'174.' I utter a sigh. Lola looks at me, trying to placate my mood.

'Our outsourced admin sets us back another four grand. Then there's four grand on top of that for the remaining admin.'

She looks right at me before I can intimate anything.

'So, after five weeks of costs and three weeks of trading, we've made eleven grand.'

'Eleven?'

'Don't forget our salaries.'

'Right.'

She can sense my disappointment with what I initially perceived as a great opening month. We're up, but watching so much cash slip away from us isn't easy.

'Have some perspective. We have $11,000 which we didn't have before, plus a grand in our pension pot. Not to mention that we still have well over a hundred grand of our start-up capital left.'

'Great.'

'May I remind you, Michael, that we only traded for three of the four weeks in November. Our cost base is largely fixed. If we'd had that extra week, we'd be looking at a six-figure profit for the month and an 11% profit margin.'

'December's going to be the same. We only have three weeks before the Christmas break.'

'Would you relax. At the very least we've got our salaries.'

'Yes, our salaries. Which give us fifty grand for the month and not ten.'

'Right. Sorry. I could use another coffee.'

My mood improves somewhat after noticing Lola's mistake.

'Fifty grand for the month. That's almost my take-home pay for the year in my old job.'

'See? And this is just the beginning.'

'I know, I know. It's just…. .'

I close my eyes, tilt my head back and exhale deeply.

'Just what?'

'I look at that pile of cash on the bed and I resent the fact that we're going to hand so much of it over to Goldstein.'

'It's temporary. This time next year we'll be free from Goldstein and that money will be ours.'

She's right.

'You're right. It's just that it's a lot of cash to let go of.'

'I get it. But think of what we can do with what we already have.'

'Yes. I owe you an engagement ring for one. A honeymoon too.'

'Damn right!'

Indeed.

'What would you say to Christmas in London? We could stay at The Ritz and spend the big day with my mother.'

'I'd love to.'

I think about Mum's ruby port-infused gravy drizzled over the Christmas dinner and enjoying a second helping while watching the Boxing Day football.

'What are you thinking about?'

Lola's curious smile is so disarming.

'Christmas dinner.'

Our warm moment is broken up by a terse knock at the door.

'That must be him.'

Lola walks over and opens the door. As predicted, it's Harley.

'Harley. So good of you to come.'

He walks right past Lola and into the room, saying nothing while wheeling a small suitcase behind him. Harley mechanically places the suitcase on the bed and unzips it while eyeing up the cash. While he does this I check my phone calendar and see a reminder of tomorrow's meeting with Redclay.

'Shit' I whisper to myself. Amid all the hoopla and excitement, we forgot to factor Redclay's December downside and November points into our calculations. We can just take it out of what remains from our start-up cash.

Harley rather methodically loads the cash into the suitcase before zipping it back up and placing it on the ground. He reaches into his left inside pocket with his right hand and pulls out a brown envelope which he blankly offers to me. I look at it for a moment, saying nothing.

'A message from Mr Goldstein. Burn after reading.'

I reach out and grip the envelope with my right hand. Harley waits several seconds before relinquishing. He shoots me an annoyed look before turning and leaving. As soon as the door closes I tear the letter from the envelope before quickly unfolding it.

'What is it?' asks Lola.

'Let me read it first.' I am slightly abrupt in my reply, which I deliver tersely before resting my eyes back on the page.

CHAPTER 32

SEVEN MONTHS LATER

It's the hottest July on record in years. The air burns like a piping furnace of colourless flames, emitting an aroma of scorched rock with no clear point of origin. A powder blue tint up above betrays the canned fire that blazes between the asphalt on the ground and the opulent glass towers on all sides.

Lola and I sit at the desk in our hotel room office with three laptop screens in front of us. The window just beyond our devices provides a clear view of the neon wilds down below. On the middle laptop screen we go over the half-year accounts, while the monitors either side give us a live feed of the action downstairs and at the Flamingo via carefully hidden cameras in the girls' purses.

The left and right hand monitors are each divided into eight equal segments, allowing us to see every inch of both bars with squares only going black when a girl leaves with a John. Each girl checks in on the group chat with the room number when she snags a client. Safety first.

'We're looking at $12 million top line revenue for the year' I exclaim with real emphasis. 'From that $12 million we're barely going to eke out a seven-figure profit. Sure, we've got our combined salary of ten grand a week, but that's nothing. All told, we're not even scraping back 5% of the gross. We've got profit and cash reserves that we can't touch. We can't reinvest it in the business, we can't pay ourselves dividends. Goldstein is killing us.'

'It's going to be another year and a half before we have enough retained earnings to pay back the remaining principal.' Lola is indignant in her reply. 'That's assuming that Goldstein is generous enough to wait until then before calling it in. Until then he's going to rinse us every month for the vig. We borrowed $3 million and, going by that timeline, we're going to end up paying back seven.'

'And what if he doesn't wait?' My reply is equally firm. 'What if he calls it in now, knowing that we don't have the cash to cover it? If we can't spring for the principal, which we can't right now, is Goldstein going to convert the debt into a controlling interest in our business?'

'We need to expand.' Lola moves her hands a lot in an animated and emphatic fashion while making her point. 'Our current business model of two locations and eight girls per, we work that so that we can pay what we owe Mr Goldstein. That's a fixed cost. Goldstein's not taking any points on the first-dollar gross. We take two more locations, and all the profits will be ours.'

I slowly shake my head and stare at the ground. This does little to halt the momentum of Hurricane Lola.

'Come on. The strip is a big place. There's one whole side where we haven't even planted our flag yet. I'm talking Mandalay Bay, Aria, MGM Grand. Our world doesn't have to begin and end with Treasure Island and Flamingo.'

'Let me get this straight, you're seriously suggesting that we take on two more locations just so that we can keep paying Goldstein what we're paying him now?'

'Hey, that's how things work in this world. It's a cost of doing business, no different from Redclay.'

'At least we're getting something out of Redclay. How many cowboys has she run off our turf already? Look at all the traffic we've gained because of the kerb crawl pickup operations she shut down outside our patches. What do we get out of the Goldstein arrangement, especially now that there's no end date in sight?'

'We get to do business in this town.'

I scoff loudly at Lola's reply and shake my head.

'Look, Michael, I hate it as much as you do. But it is what it is.'

'You're right.'

Lola looks at me with an air of genuine surprise.

'It is what it is until we make it not so. I agreed to pay back the debt in good faith. Hell, we even gave him a million dollars up front. What more does he want?'

'There's no such thing as in good faith in this business.'

I look right at Lola. Her comment hits me like a reality punch to the gut.

'You opened this door to keep Harley from killing Nile, and he's dead anyway. We're on the other side of that door now and Goldstein is holding the only key.'

'Don't you put this on me! Goldstein switched up the terms.... .'

'He can switch up the terms whenever he likes!'

Lola is very blunt and matter of fact. Her words ring very true with the harsh realities of this world.

'You're right. You're exactly right. And that is why we cannot stay in his pocket.'

'This is a necessary evil. We make enough money and this won't matter.'

We're going around in circles. It's hopeless.

'I'm all for expanding, but for us and not for him. How do we know he won't shift the goalposts again?'

'What do you suggest?'

'Instead of waiting for Goldstein to call in the principal, we call it in for him.'

'Are you out of your mind?'

'No. Not at all. Keeping this madness with Goldstein going a minute longer than we have to, which we already have, is what is crazy.'

'So what's the plan, you're going to shove the two million into Jeremy Goldstein's hands and tell him what's what? Besides, where are we going to get the two million from? You going to shake the money tree? Get the girls to waive their commission? May I remind you that we barely have half a million dollars in the bank right now.'

'I'm very much aware of our current cash flow situation, seeing as I am the CFO of the company.'

'And I am the COO and your co-CEO. As such, I don't support this course of action.'

I look at Lola gruffly and say nothing.

'If we give him the principal then from that moment on he's losing his precious vig.'

'I've already thought about that. We put a cherry on top. Six months of interest plus the two million to sweeten the pot and break free from this bullshit debt to Goldstein.'

'He won't take too kindly to you cutting him out of several more months, possibly even years, of further vig.'

'He can go shit in his hat then.'

Lola looks at the ground, silently laughing and shaking her head.

'We're doing business in his city, so we gotta pay tax.'

'He's not even into vice. His primary interest is narcotics.'

'Get real. Everybody else running any kind of street game in this town is kicking up tribute to Goldstein. Loan sharking, numbers, sports books. Besides, you made it his business.'

'Alright. Alright.'

'Anyway, how are we going to get $2 million plus your cherry on top together just like that?'

I hit a few keys on the laptop before punching enter with my right index finger in a slightly ostentatious manner. The internet search page quickly updates to a barrage of gaudy colours and font scattered between photo-enhanced faces.

'Wrestling?'

'Yes.'

'I don't get it.'

'We have an opportunity here. We're not going to miss it.'

CHAPTER 33

Whatever happened to my dreams? When I typed them up for my university yearbook entry was I also writing a ticket of my youthful ambition, one that would inevitably get punched in return for boring, stifling stability? Five years from graduation I wanted to be working and living in Toronto, en route to my first million. Eight years on and I'm a million miles from both.

Every single day I think about how different my life would be right now if I'd rolled the dice at 21. Staked my claim in the world of investment banking when that door was wide open before me. But here I am, watching the last flush of that young fire die with every flash of blue light from the photocopier.

90 days from now I'll be in Las Vegas. A sweet escape from the humdrum and tedium that is now my life. Once the West Coast adventure is over I'm going to commit every single waking hour that I'm not here to getting out. It doesn't matter how tired or bored or frustrated or lonely I get along the way. I will do whatever it takes to break free and be the person I was meant to be.

Does anybody truly fulfil their dreams, or are we all just meandering along in a faded version of our ideal just to keep our place in somebody else's race?

Saturday night. Hakassan is a dark blur of strobe lights, bodies and sparks flying from bottle sparklers in all directions. Lola and I, along with our sixteen-strong squad of girls, occupy a VIP section, the table before us lined with bottles of all hues as well as various savoury nibbles. Lola and I smoke Cuban cigars while knocking back Buckler. The girls sip club soda and bop to the music, with only Mona and Gabriella partaking in the Havanas with us.

Across the club from us in another VIP area just like ours. Holding court and standing tall with a bottle of Cristal in each hand, black Stetson on his head to boot, is our target. Brad Thunberg. The wrestler. The World Heavyweight Champion. Even surrounded by half a dozen other beefed-up grapplers, he stands out and is truly a specimen to behold.

At 6 ft 4 in and 270lb with short blonde hair, piercing blue eyes and matinee idol features, the self-proclaimed Hillbilly Jew Barbarian has all eyes on him. Nobody outside of his circle has been able to get past his velvet rope and bouncers so far. Many of the clubbers here fell in from the neighbouring MGM Grand Garden Arena after seeing Thunberg's latest successful title defence.

An undefeated amateur wrestler with a NCAA Championship and Olympic gold medal to his name, Thunberg next set his sights on MMA, racking up fifteen consecutive wins over five years and breaking all kinds of PPV and gate records before retiring with the Heavyweight Championship. After seeing the breadth of his domain in the octagon, professional wrestling provided a new challenge. Little more than a year after his debut and he's one year into a blockbuster tile reign. All this at just 30 years old.

Last year Brad Thunberg earned a reported $20 million, and this year is shaping up to be even better. In addition to a new 10-year wrestling contract paying him a guaranteed $30 million and various endorsements, Thunberg is currently looking at big money options in both Hollywood and boxing.

I look over the girls from left to right, contemplating my next move. So far everything has gone according to plan. Our army of tipsters told us where the party would be and when. Now it's up to us the deploy the heavy artillery.

'What's the plan now?' whispers Lola beneath the ear-pounding beats.

If all goes to plan from here, Thunberg's glittering career with be in our hands in just a few hours and the cash we need to pay off Goldstein will be within touching distance.

'I'm just thinking who would be best for this job.'

'I've got an idea. Once the trap's sprung how about we head on out of here and grab a little dessert at Planet Hollywood? We leave the rest of the girls to do their thing and we get ready for the next phase of the plan.'

'Sounds good.'

'I guess we better decide then.'

Even at this crazy hour, Lola's determination doesn't let up.

'Alright.'

She looks at me as if to say 'Five minutes ago would be great.'

'I go Gabriella.'

'Gabriella it is.'

I look over to Gabriella, clad in a dark blue dress which perfectly hugs every bountiful curve of her hourglass figure, and gesture with two figures on my right hand.

'Gabriella!'

The loud music downs out my cry.

'Gabby!'

She looks over and puts her glass down before slowly walking across to us.

'You're up' I say while pointing and turning my head towards Thunberg.

'I got this.'

I pat Gabriella on the back twice with my left hand. As she takes off Lola gives her curvy behind a playful jock slap. Gabriella's walk is one of confidence and power, of a woman who has mastered her destiny and could master yours too if she so chose.

The other girls look on with a real fervour, as if they're watching a huge sporting event. Two burly bouncers in dark suits put on stern faces and are initially reluctant to let Gabriella pass, only relenting when Thunberg leans over and whispers something to them. One of the bouncers proceeds to unclip the velvet rope and our girl nonchalantly struts into Thunberg's waiting arms.

Gabriella whispers something to Thunberg, who arches down so he can hear her properly. He grins and goofily nods his head upon hearing what she has to say. After whispering something back which makes Gabriella laugh, Thunberg stands back upright and begins elaborately gesticulating to a waiter with his right hand.

Thunberg stops the waiter just before the velvet rope and slips a C-note into his top pocket. They chat for several seconds before the waiter leaves. An ebullient Thunberg takes a slow lap of the VIP with Gabriella hanging from his right harm, the two of them chatting and laughing at each stop with Thunberg high-fiving each of his boys for good measure. Once the last of the flesh has been pressed, he pats on a bouncer's broad shoulder and whispers something to him. The bouncer nods his head before turning around to unclip the rope and lead the pair towards the exit.

'We've got him' I lean over and whisper to Lola.

'Hook, line and sinker.' Lola can't stop beaming. The girls behind us are in great form and are all genuinely happy for Gabriella. We clink bottles as *Ibiza* by Mike Posner begins to play. Without a care in the world we begin to sing the words to one another.

'I took a pill in Ibiza.'

'To show Avicii I was cool.'

'And when I finally got sober, I felt ten years older.'

'But fuck it, it was something to do.'

I turn around and begin mock conducting the girls.

'I'm living out on LA.'

'I drive a sportscar just to prove.'

'I'm a real big baller, 'cause I made a million dollars.'

'And I spent it on girls and shoes.'

CHAPTER 34

Lola and I are sitting in bed watching an edited version of *The Hangover* on TNT. From the first time I saw this film at the age of 16 I dreamed of having my bachelor party in Las Vegas. Back then even the idea of a girlfriend was preposterous. Shockingly the boys in drama club, cookery club and textiles club didn't get all the girls.

All the plot beats are the same as the previous umpteen occasions on which I've seen this film. However, this being early morning viewing, many of the best jokes are quite different. 'Shit' becomes 'Smokes' and Mr Chow's oft-imitated catchphrase of sorts now refers to 'Cowboys' rather than 'Gayboys.'

As the film goes for a commercial break I turn to my left and see my phone lit up with notifications of texts, missed calls, WhatsApp messages and news alerts which I've ignored until now. One alert in particular catches my eye with a photo of Brad Thunberg, the very man we'll be shaking down for millions just hours from now, in the thumbnail.

'BREAKING NEWS: Wrestling Champion Brad Thunberg & Female Companion Hospitalized Following Las Vegas Car Crash.'

'Oy vey!'

I roll out of bed and grab the phone, ignoring Lola's pleas on my way to the bathroom. After locking the door behind myself I return to the phone and click on the thumbnail. Lola pounds on the door rather anxiously but I don't respond.

The thumbnail takes me to a gaudy celebrity gossip site with links to ads for dating sites promising beautiful Slavic women and one of those top 10 lists of useless celebrity trivia. That same headline jumps off the screen in bold black font, twisting a horrible truth hard into my mind.

Beneath a blurb of ominous words is a full colour photo of a bright blue Mustang turned upside down and surrounded by broken glass, crashed through the window of a CVS Pharmacy. The words either side of the image are largely a blur, only the likes of 'speeding', 'cocaine' and 'collision' really hitting me at first.

Between a lot of hyperbole and aggrandisement regarding Thunberg and his numerous accomplishments there's a vague mention of an 'unidentified female companion'. Apparently the 911 call came at 03:04, little over two hours after we sent Gabriella to Thunberg. I open the bathroom door to be met by an alarmed and confused Lola.

'What the fuck?'

That's alarmed and confused right there.

'We need to start calling around to hospitals. It looks like Gabriella was in a car accident.'

'What?'

'A crash. Apparently, Thunberg got high and crashed through the front window of a CVS Pharmacy.'

'Motherfucker!'

Indeed.

'Let's call Redclay first. She must know something by now.'

'Indeed.'

Lola walks across and grabs her phone from the bedside table before frantically punching keys.

'Come on Redclay, answer!'

Lola is becoming increasingly agitated and throws the phone to the bead after it goes to voicemail.

'Fuck!'

'Come on. Let's think. Where would they have been taken?'

'We should try the UMC on West Charleston Boulevard first.'

'Isn't that the hospital where Tupac Shakur died?'

Lola shoots me a look of frustration and I immediately regret my choice of words.

'Sorry.'

'Just forget it.'

'I'm calling an Uber. You stay here with Jennifer. I've got this.'

'Keep me posted and let me know once you reach Redclay. We need her help to keep us out of the line of fire here.'

'Right.'

I pull up the Uber app and start tapping UMC West Charleston Boulevard. Confirmed. Now looking for a driver.

Looking.

Looking.

Still looking.

'Come on, come on.'

The black line keeps running along the screen from left to right. A red dot flashes on the map above marking the spot of my destination. A flash runs along the orange line marking out the route of the journey. It's an agonizing wait, like staring at a broken record hoping it will play sweet music once again.

'Fuck this shit!'

After a few more seconds the screen blinks and the image changes rather suddenly. Bogdan will be my driver.

'Six minutes. Six minutes.'

I return to the bathroom and lean my back against the door behind me, trying to process what's happening. Stilted breaths begin to zip through my lungs faster than my mouth and nose can stand. Every other gasp begins to hurt my chest and throat. I pull my phone closer to my face and start trawling through the barrage of unread messages in the group chat, only for the phone screen to sharply freeze and fade to black.

'Shit! Shit! Shit!'

The back of my head bangs against the bathroom door. No time to brood. Need to run outside and catch my Uber after failing to make a mental note of the make, model, or plate number. I'll just have to stare at and flag down random cars looking for Bogdan. I place my phone by the bathtub before briskly turning to leave the bathroom.

I race past the bed and hurriedly throw on my jacket from the hook on the back of the door on my way out. Without looking at or listening to anything or anyone I scurry through the hallway and out the front door.

Past apartment A308 on my left and through a single door straight ahead. Another door to my left leads to the lift and stairwell. I hit the button with my right hand. It lights up red but doesn't move. After a few seconds I give up and start galloping down the stairs, only just now realising that I'm wearing only mismatched socks on my feet.

Second floor. First floor. Ground. Round the end on the right and straight through the exit. I race over to a bright red Toyota Yaris pulling up outside the building and grab onto the door.

'Bogdan? Bogdan?'

The middle-aged driver looks at me without saying anything before briskly driving away.

'Bloody phone! Of all the times for it to crap out on me!'

I look around frantically at cars passing in both directions, with not even the slightest clue as to what I'm looking for.

'Gordon Bennett!'

I turn around and see a green Ford Taurus slowly inch out from left to right around a corner in the foreground. The driver looks to his left and in front but not right towards me.

'Hey!' I shout with my right hand raised in the air before rushing over. I tap on the window with one knuckle, prompting him to turn and face me.

'You Bogdan?'

'Uh-huh. What you want, university hospital?'

CHAPTER 35

The lobby of the hospital is a dull and clinical space at odds with the lurid veneer of the strip. Seats are piled from end to end largely with the bodies of young men and women, no doubt paying for last night's misadventures with what will one day serve as a funny yet slightly macabre anecdote. From my left I vaguely overhear a conversation among three men and a doctor, standing around discussing how one of the men was bitten by a sex worker.

I turn to the right and look across to the reception area before walking over. Out of the corner of my left eye a uniformed police officer rests against a column, talking into his phone while looking around carefully every few seconds.

'Get this Roy: The female victim is Oana Raduciou. A.K.A. Emily. Didn't she work for that scumbag who fell off the face of the Earth last year? Yeah, Raven, Goldstein's bitch.'

Raduciou? Our records show Emily's real name as being Orsela Proval. Why would she use an alias? And what's going on? Gabriella was in the car with Thunberg, yet somehow Emily is here and laid up in a hospital bed, injured.

I get a look at the gold name pin attached to the cop's black shirt. Officer Muldoon. I'll have to run that name by Redclay later on. Need to know who he is, who he was talking to about Goldstein and what. Goldstein's business is a little above his pay grade. I also need to ask Redclay about Emily.

I turn away from the reception desk and dart outside. Once Muldoon is gone, I can go back and ask about Emily. But what about Gabriella? What the hell happened?

As the automatic doors of the entrance close behind me I'm greeted by the sight of Gabriella in the distance. Her long brown hair is tied back into a ponytail and she's wearing a black leather jacket, plain white T-shirt and right blue jeans. Holding a Starbucks cup in her right hand as she approaches the front of the hospital, there isn't a scratch on Gabriella.

'Gabby?'

I signal to her to stop with my right hand before hastening my walk. Upon reaching Gabriella I gently take her right arm in my left hand and lead her around the corner to the right.

'What happened with Thunberg?'

'Long story.'

'I've got nothing but time. Start talking.'

Gabriella brushes her air out of her face and gently sighs. She is visibly tired and in no mood to talk.

'After we left the club, we got to his suite. Drank champagne, fooled around a little. Then suddenly Thunberg asks if I have a friend who would want in, so I call Emily.'

'Alright.'

'Emily gets to the room and we drink some more, Emily and I make out a little while he watches and we spin some tunes. It was all good until Brad broke out a huge bag of blow and starting snorting. He was hoovering that shit up like Scarface and he started acting all crazy when he was high.'

'Did you girls hit the white powder too?'

'No. Fuck no.'

'Please tell me you at least got paid?'

'Are you fucking serious? Emily is in a coma right now.'

I look right at Gabriella and say nothing, prompting an irritated scoff.

'Of course we did. Thunberg gave us ten grand each.'

'That's off the books. It's all yours.'

'Least of my worries right now. I've put my ten grand aside to help with Emily's medical bills just in case the insurance doesn't pay out. All of the girls are throwing in. We're taking it in turns to see Emily and take care of her stuff at home. You know, her rent, bills and all of that.'

'Right.'

'She sends a MoneyGram home to her mum and kid brother in Bucharest every week. The little man wants to be a mechanical engineer. We're going to keep that going while she's in hospital and throw in some cash of our own to make up any shortfall.'

'We'll take care of her too. Medical bills, insurance or not, anything else she has going on. We've got her.'

Gabriella smiles faintly at this.

'So, what happened after Thunberg got high?'

'He ran out of blow and kept asking us to go out and score with him. I took Emily to the bathroom, told her we should leave right away but she wouldn't do it. Said one of us needed to stay so we could get the footage.'

'Shit.'

'I told her you'd understand.'

I do, but my understanding won't get us out of the Goldstein-shaped hole that we're in.

'Of course. Totally.'

I'm stuck in a weird space between compassion for the injured Emily and our own plight after a plan which didn't come together.

'So, you left and she stayed?'

'Er, yeah.'

'She stayed and went out to score with him. Shit!'

'I didn't want either of us with him while he was all high and loopy, but I couldn't drag Emily out of that suite. She insisted on getting that footage. Plus she thought there would be a nice tip on top of the ten grand.'

I'm proud of how close the girls have grown to one another. The way they watch one another's backs is remarkable. If Emily dies the other girls will be devastated.

'What did the doctors say?'

'Emily has a severe bleed to the brain. Several broken ribs, a collapsed lung, ruptured kidney, internal bleeding. If she does survive this, she won't be the same again. At least not for a very long time.'

'Lola and I will take care of Emily and her family in the long run. No matter what.'

'You're a good man. Lola is lucky to have you.'

'Actually, I'm the lucky one. Being with Lola has made me a much better person.'

Gabriella looks at me with a sweet, honest earnestness in her eyes. I see the tears forming and go in to hug her. She throws her arms around me and clasps my back tightly.

'This is all my fault. I should have made Emily leave that room.'

Gabriella begins to audibly sob as she presses her face into my chest while digging the balls of her fingers into my back.

'No.'

I kiss her on the dome and rub the back of her head.

'This is on Thunberg. Him and him alone. If he survives this, we're going to make him pay.'

CHAPTER 36

I stand on the corner waiting for Redclay after calling her from Gabriella's phone. I'm far enough from the hospital entrance to avoid being seen by Muldoon if he emerges, but close enough to see him come out at a squint. As soon as I'm sure that he's gone I'll go and check on Emily.

Redclay's car pulls up and I get in next to her. She turns off the stereo to give me her full attention.

'Sorry I couldn't make it down until now. I heard what happened. Been slammed for hours with John busts at the Motel 6.'

'Anyway, we're both here now.'

'What do you need?'

'I need you to run two names for me.'

'OK. The first one?'

'Officer Muldoon. A uniform in your department.'

'Ben Muldoon. Patrol. What do you need to know?'

'He's working this. I need to know what exactly his angle is. He was on the phone talking to someone about Raven and Goldstein. He knows that Emily worked for Raven, and that Raven worked for Goldstein.'

'Why would that interest a lowly patrolman?'

'I need you to put eyes on him and find out. What concerns me the most is the person on the other end of that call. Who was it and what's their angle?'

'Give me a week and I'll rustle up some answers.'

'You've got four days.'

'Fine. And the second name?'

'Oana Raduciou.'

'Who's that?'

'It's Emily's real name.'

'Why do you care about that?'

'It's not the name she gave us. I need to know why she lied. Muldoon knows her real name. What else does he know that we don't?'

'I hear ya.'

'What's to stop Muldoon and his mystery partner from connecting Emily to us?'

The irony here is that Emily's alias is the only thing stopping Muldoon from connecting Emily to us right now. If she had given us her real name, the one he has in his little black notebook, Muldoon would be onto us as I speak.

'You have Emily on your books under an alias.'

Yes. I just said that.

'There's no paper trail connecting her joy ride with Thunberg to Top Drawer.'

'But if he gets her fingerprints he can run them through every database in the land. Emily has a driver's license under the name she gave us. Once Muldoon makes the connection we'll have eyes on us like we've never had before.'

'Fuck.'

You can say that again.

'Even if they make that connection there's nothing they can do. They can't prove that you set Emily up with Thunberg without a money trail. All they can do is watch.'

'I don't want the heat.'

'You dipped your toes in the furnace. There's going to be heat once in a while. Heat comes and goes. They find nothing, they do nothing, they fuck off for a while.'

'Right.'

Her words give me no assurance whatsoever.

'I'll run those names tonight.'

'Do it.'

'So where's Lola?'

'At home with our daughter.'

'When did she become your daughter?'

'When I married her mother and moved in.'

Diana quietly smiles and gives me an admiring look.

'What happened to her real father?'

'I'm here, he's not. That's real enough.'

'Right.'

'I need you to do one more thing for me.'

'And what's that?'

'Call something in to get Muldoon out of here.'

'Like what?'

'I don't know. Say there's a cat up a tree or something.'

'Funny.'

'Just get him out of here so I can see Emily.'

Diana flashes me a hard look before reaching for the radio.

'All patrol units required. 142 at the MGM Grand. Need a location for Officer Muldoon. Over.'

'142?'

'Unlawful assembly.'

'I see.'

We sit in silence while waiting for a response. I'm hoping the cops are a little faster here than they are in London.

'You should have said we'd found Jimmy Hoffa's remains.'

'Ha.'

'It's funny how he disappeared just like that.'

'Kinda like Jimmy and Buford.'

Yeah. Amazing how this world went from being something we heard and read about to becoming our new reality.

'Did they ever find out who whacked Hoffa?' I ask despite already knowing the answer, my desperation to change the subject being so painfully obvious.

'You don't believe it was Frank Sheeran?'

'About as much as I believe it was Ed Sheeran.'

'I won't tell Scorsese you said that.'

'Great movie, don't get me wrong, but I call bullshit. I can maybe buy that he killed Joey Gallo, but no way did he knock of Hoffa.'

'You'd be surprised by what some people have done.'

Bitch.

'Let's go to Taco Bell while we wait. You're buying.'

CHAPTER 37

Lola, Jennifer and I sit in Ghiradelli enjoying hot fudge sundaes and looking just like any other family there. Jennifer sits across from us excitedly drawing a picture of various toys and cartoon characters which she colours in with slim felt tip pens. She's a genuinely bright and happy child, a real light in my life. I'm very proud of her.

'That's really cool. Who's that one there?' I ask while pointing to a pink figure in Jennifer's drawing with my right index finger.

'That's George.'

'George?'

'Yep. He's Peppa Pig's brother.'

'I didn't know Peppa had a brother.'

'Peppa and George do everything together.'

'That's great.'

'I want a little brother just like George.'

Lola and I look at one another and smile. If words could melt my heart, those words certainly would.

'I know.'

I take my right hand and rub Lola's cheek, causing her to coyly smile and quietly purr in response with her eyes closed.

'You keep being a good girl and Mummy and I will see what we can do.'

'Yay!'

Jennifer's joyful youthful jollity is hard to resist. I never thought a moment like this could ever do it for me, but a lot of things which I previously never imagined possible have come to fruition over the last several months. This right here is without a doubt the sweetest. I now have a family. Something worth preserving. Something priceless. Something real.

'I've got an idea. How about after we finish up here we go and ride the High Roller?'

'Yay! I wanna go! I wanna go!'

My phone rings. I reach over with my right hand to see who it is. It's Diana.

'I need to take this. I'll be right back.'

I get up from the table and head for the facilities. After stopping and carefully looking around I open the door to the disabled toilet and let myself in. With my left hand I click the door locked before answering the phone with my right.

'Diana. What took you so long?'

'Hello to you too.'

'Yeah yeah. What you got for me?'

'Seems Emily has been a naughty girl. She's almost two years into a three-year probation for a nightclub stabbing in Miami.'

'As stabbing?'

'Yeah. Apparently it was a dispute over $500.'

'Shit. One of our girls on probation is going to be a problem. A huge problem. If she gets popped for anything we're going to lose her to the Nevada Department of Corrections.'

'Your benefits package doesn't include bail money?'

'Funny.'

'Besides, you're assuming that she'll get convicted if she gets pinched. Not everyone has a Sergeant on the inside who can bury a case at will. But you do.'

'Right.'

'I thought that would fill you with more confidence that that.'

'I know what I need to know about Emily. What about Muldoon?'

'Nothing yet. Drips and drabs, but nothing concrete.'

'You've got until Wednesday night.'

I hang up. For sure I should have been more diplomatic, especially given what Redclay knows, but a rush of blood to the head got the better of me. If Emily comes around and finds herself staring at a solicitation charge, what will stop her giving us up to stay out of jail? What if Redclay for whatever reason can't bury the charges? Muldoon's unknown friend throws an unknown into the equation which could be beyond our control.

Everything around me begins to blur. I can hear the staccato beating of my heart and small breaths which usually don't make a sound. The echo of each heartbeat hits my ears hard while the feeling quickly drains from my arms. All shapes and colours in the periphery are bent out of focus and a grainy black falls over my view.

My legs give way and before I can feel anything below a cloak of black engulfs everything in front of my eyes.

The midday hour. This is the absolute highlight of my day. Just me, my Tesco meal deal, a good book and, if a creative purple patch calls for it, my trusted pad and pen. An hour free from the obnoxious noise coming from the sewing circle in Accounts Payable. This morning's highlight was a thought-provoking discussion about Dostoyevsky, largely centred around how relatively unappreciated *The Gambler* is and how much of the critique of the prison system laid out in *House of The Dead* is still valid today.

Of course not. The latest bout of inane squawking from what the company's General Manager calls the frivolous side of the department was something or other to do with Antonio Banderas. So frivolous that the company don't let them go, despite their obvious detriment to the business. It's amazing what can be achieved when one is sleeping with the boss.

Little more than 60 days to go now. San Francisco, then Los Angeles, and finally Las Vegas. How great would it be if I hit the West Coast trail and just kept going, never to return? It's a nice thought but that's all it is and all it ever will be. That's not what I do, letting go of one rung without a firm grip on the next one.

The best that I can hope for is that this awesome trip will provide me with some amazing memories, the kind I can reach for as a reminder of what is truly possible when the humdrum of everyday life begins to eat at me again.

Eight years ago I had the brass ring in my sights just waiting for me but I opted for the safety of the lemon in my hand. That opportunity never came around again.

Today between bites of my smoked ham and cheddar sandwich I lose myself in the words of Charles Bukowski. I turn over the face of my watch to avoid reminders of the time falling off the face of the day. The 1pm alarm will break my solitude soon enough.

Bukowski's words enrapture me in a haze of cigarette burns and whisky-soaked viscera. His beautiful gutter verse brings to life the harsh and mundane realities of concrete jungle life. The love-hate relationship with what we do have and the constant pursuit of the things we never will possess.

I sometimes think about the life of one of these old louche poets. There's a certain romance in that rootless vagabond existence. One which lends itself to the greatest of great art. So far from the same train ride, the same desk, the same faces every single day.

Every single word speaks to me, like an aggressive call to arms urging me to reach inside of myself for something true, something greater. The voice inspires like that of Mr Keating but with the venom and bombast of Gunnery Sergeant Hartman. At 1pm when my alarm goes off I will rush to the next full stop, close my book and return to my desk. In that respect I'm a lot like the people who are healed in church on Sunday only to be broken again halfway through their Monday.

Oh to make my perfect midday hour permanent.

CHAPTER 38

Sitting in the hospital waiting room next to Lola. I have only a vague recollection of how I got here. Clipped flashes of the back of a cab. Trump's resort standing like a lone gold bar on the Strip refracting the sun. A UFC billboard prominently displaying two faces I don't recognize. The last thing I can clearly remember is the disabled bathroom in Ghiradelli turning upside down.

13 Going on 30 plays on a TV screen mounted high to the wall directly opposite me. Not a movie I ever planned to see. For some strange reason I am struck by the presence of Mark Ruffalo in this film.

'What are we doing here?'

'You had a fall in the bathroom back at Ghiradelli. After you were gone twenty minutes, I got the manager to open it up and check on you.'

'A fall?'

'Yeah. You were out like a light.'

'Where's Jennifer?'

'I dropped her off at Olivia's place.'

'OK.'

Lola takes my left hand in her right and squeezes it gently yet rather playfully.

'What happened to my sundae?'

This prompts a quiet laugh from Lola.

'Forget your sundae. We need to get you checked out.'

'When we're out of here you're buying me another sundae.'

'You're obviously fine, but you're seeing the doctor all the same. I'll even make it two sundaes.'

'You've got a deal.'

'Cool.'

Lola smiles after I place a gentle kiss on her right cheek. The credits roll on the movie nobody was watching.

'How do you feel right now?'

'A lot better, I must say, except for the fact that I can't remember much of what happened earlier. Well enough to be out of here, so come on. Let's bounce.'

'Not a chance. Hold your horses, cowboy! You probably have a concussion, so we really need to get you checked out.'

'Oh alright then.'

Watermelon Sugar by Harry Styles begins to play over the stereo. The opening lyrics prompt Lola to rest her head on my shoulder.

'Strawberries on a summer evening. That sounds like a plan.'

'Let's swing by Walgreens later on.'

'You're on.'

'Sundaes and strawberries. I can think of one more S that would make for a perfect trifecta.'

'Me too. I noticed that *Scarface* is on TV later on.'

Classic Lola. I love this woman.

'I love you.'

'I love you too.'

The song plays on and we quietly sing the words to one another. Moments like this bring sweet light to this tunnel of chaos which is the world we chose.

'Before we go home we should check on Emily.' I knew from the first moment I saw Lola that she was one of the sweet ones.

'Absolutely.'

13 Going on 30 starts again on the TV. Oh joy.

'I need to go to the bathroom.'

After quickly kissing Lola on the lips I get up and begin making my way towards the men's room on the right beyond the reception area. While glancing at the TV on the left I feel a firm torso sharply collide with mine.

'I'm terribly sorry.'

'That's quite alright' replies the gentleman. It's Office Muldoon.

'Nice glasses. What does that say on the side, Land Rover?'

I see a Detective shield in Officer Muldoon's future.

'Yes.'

'Interesting.'

It really isn't.

'I guess so.'

Muldoon walks off towards the reception desk as I look on. His attention to detail has unnerved me somewhat.

'Officer Muldoon, Las Vegas Metro' he says while flashing his badge to the young blonde receptionist. 'I'm going to need the names of all visitors for Oana Raduciou. Can I get a list?'

'Shit!'

I pace towards the disabled facilities and lock the door hard after letting myself in.

'This is bad.'

The list will contain mine and Lola's names as well as those of our employees. Half of our girls worked for Raven, long-time courier and burgeoning distributor to one Jeremy Goldstein. Whoever Muldoon was talking to on the phone the other day will instantly make the connection and we'll become collateral damage in whatever comes Goldstein's way.

Time to call Diana.

'Fuck.'

I call Redclay. One ring. Two rings. Three rings.

'Hey. I'm guessing you didn't call to ask me to a movie.'

'Listen Diana, just listen. What I said before about Muldoon, forget it. We need to move on him right now.'

'What do you mean right now?'

'We need to move on him before he and his mystery pal move on us. He's made me, Lola, and all of our employees. Soon enough he'll connect us to Raven and Goldstein beyond just Emily. We have to move on him tonight.'

'Look, Michael, if you're going to insist on hunting down everybody who looks at you the wrong way then you're going to have to start paying me more. Muldoon's a small-timer, always trying to dip his toes where they don't belong. He helped Homicide on a case three years ago, thought it was going to be his golden ticket out of Patrol and onto the fast track to making Detective.'

Interesting.

'He got a glowing performance review but as soon as the case broke, he was dumped back on the beat. Since then he's been looking for another career-maker, but nothing so far.'

'So you found all of this out but didn't mention it until now?'

'I was going to give you all the info once I'd finished digging. I'm not done yet.'

'Now you are. The next digging that will be done as far as Muldoon is concerned will be for his hole in the desert.'

'Jesus!'

'Jesus has got nothing to do with it! However, I am interested in whoever was on the other end of his phone call.'

'Probably another nobody with no real clout. Small potatoes. Amateur sleuthing.'

'I'm not taking that chance. No way. Make a few calls, round up some gangbangers who owe you a favour and make it happen. Call me when you've got him someplace quiet so we can talk. Just me. No Lola.'

'This is nuts.'

'And I don't want to hear from you until it's done.'

CHAPTER 39

Home alone today. Not my idea. It turns out that I did suffer a minor concussion. Lola has benched me for the rest of the week as a precaution. Jennifer is in day care while Lola runs things from our Treasure Island office. I'm here on the living room couch engaging in my new and rather unorthodox creative process: writing poetry while spinning a *Moesha* marathon on Netflix.

It's definitely odd but it works all the same. I never really watched the show before but I've pretty much always known about Brandy. Moesha's two gal pals, Niecy and Kim, are hilarious. I'm not quite sure why Hakeem always eats at the Mitchells' house, but I do remember him mentioning how he would make cheese on toast with the cheese going into the toaster if he had said toaster. Or cheese. Or bread. That actually made me sad.

Already I'm amazed by how much having an ostensibly irrelevant show on in the background can aid the creative process. It's coming up to 1pm and I'm enjoying a real purple patch creatively. This morning yielded some of my best and most powerful work ever. In fact, one piece I wrote this morning might just be my absolute best.

Brianna (MMIW)

I am not your cause celebre du jour
Nor the anachronistic sombre hashtag
Between the gaudy glitz and glamour
Of your vainglorious digital life kernels
I was a daughter, sister, aunt and friend
A youthful mass of burgeoning dreams
The ceiling shadow cast by the empty chair
Now a mausoleum of a life less lived
I am one of the six thousand
But not of the three hundred
And not of the fifteen
Who briefly sojourn in the fickle lexicon
I was the runaway who would come back
Yet never did
My case never opened
My story never told
I long to be a staple
In your everyday language
So the spirit of my sisters
Can live long beyond their suffering.

The idea came to me while I was re-watching *Dexter: New Blood* with Lola a few weeks ago. Missing and Murdered Indigenous Women came up and I was once again reminded of a news item I came across in 2015. A report about Native American women being raped by non-Natives on reservations and, due to those reservations effectively being sovereign nations, law enforcement not having the jurisdiction to prosecute the perpetrators.

Suddenly I got to thinking about Brianna, a beautiful and charming young lady working at the Grand Canyon gift shop. She served me when I bought my beloved cowboy hat. I met Brianna just hours before my fateful trip to Sapphires. The MMIW subject hits home harder than ever now that I have a part-Taino wife and daughter.

Lola wandered into a dangerous world but she will never be alone in that realm ever again. I'll never let any harm come to Lola or Jennifer and I'll ensure that it never does by any means necessary. Occupying a lane so inherently ruthless will call for some nefarious means from time to time, but we've both been there already. Once a line drawn in blood has been crossed it sears itself into your psyche indelibly, to the point where you become the other side and crossing back over is redundant.

No word yet from Redclay. She followed my words to the letter. At least the part about how I didn't want to hear from her again until she had rounded up Muldoon. Unfortunately, she doesn't appear to have acted on my instruction to get him last night. I know she didn't agree with my request but we're paying her to protect our interests as we see fit.

Going after a cop like this is next level. There are so many ways in which this could go sideways, but the consequences of doing nothing could be far worse. Our plan to blackmail Brad Thunberg fell apart and has put us firmly in the line of fire. We can't just stand around waiting for the first bullet to be fired and hoping it misses the mark.

Whoever Muldoon was on the phone to could be planning some terrible things for us. What if he's sleuthing at the behest of one of Goldstein's rivals? He could be just as dirty as Redclay, a terrifying prospect for an adversary. Muldoon is or was a jobsworth who did everything right yet he didn't get what was coming to him. I now know better than most how that kind of disappointment can push someone beyond the threshold of their moral possibilities. That push can make one dangerous and change the very fabric of who they are.

I'm no longer the accountant who boarded that flight from Heathrow to San Francisco last October, watching *Goodfellas* and eating pretzels while airborne. Nor am I the man who looked on awestruck at the Las Vegas lights. I'm not even the man who married Lola on a whim one night. That was just the beginning. The events of that trip changed me forever. That can't be denied.

It's amazing how something as frivolous as a *Moesha* marathon can provide the backdrop to the writing of such powerful words. Then again it was a holiday with the boys, one which I seriously considered skipping out on a few months beforehand, which gave rise to our $1 million per month criminal empire.

That empire is currently at a standstill. We agreed to give the girls the week off in light of what happened to Emily on Saturday. One whole week of losing money and having to reach into our cash reserves for Goldstein's vig. Our territory is now open to new players. They may have an inferior offering to ours, but right now we're not there. The underdogs can see the trophy clearly in the distance once the holders have been knocked out.

The shutdown was Lola's call, not mine. It may have been the right thing to do from a compassion standpoint, sure. But this is a world where compassion and mercy present deadly adversaries with opportunity.

Yes, the Thunberg mess that got us here was my call, but there is no justification for making no money at all. Between the loss of revenue, taking care of Emily and what we owe Goldstein, we're in something of a bind. Lola has already shot down my proposal to increase the billing hours quota for next week, to double it from 16 hours per head to thirty-two. We need to expand, even if it means depleting our ringfenced cash reserves. Concussion or not, I can't just sit here.

I have half a mind to get out of here and head to Sapphires, do a little recruiting. But every single time I get up off the sofa to get a beer from the fridge I feel nausea and a piercing headache. Part of me wants to just pound down an energy drink and suck it up, yet each time that pain hits my head like an errant splinter of glass all thoughts of going beyond the front door quickly dissolve.

I'm staring at my phone watching the minutes on the clock hold still when an idea suddenly comes to mind. We need more girls, a whole new team to service a whole new location. Maybe even two new spots. The plan was always to expand but recent events have forced our hand, especially now that Lola is talking about giving the girls next week off as well.

A $512,000 hole where there should be revenue is quite frankly unacceptable. So too is Lola's suggestion that the two of us temporarily defer our salaries. Yes, this situation with Emily is very sad and unfortunate, but at the end of the day we live in a world of commercial realities both good and bad.

Compassionate leave. Aptly named because Lola's compassionate nature will leave us over a million dollars short if one week off becomes two. We're already paying these girls guaranteed money and providing them with benefits and seven weeks per year of paid holiday. None of the gangbanger wannabe pimps out there would give them that. This was also Lola's call. Every single step of the way.

I'm going to drop a message in the group chat for the girls. Maybe I can't hit the strip clubs and recruit, but they can. I'm going to offer a $1,000 recruitment/referral bonus for each new girl who passes her probation, plus a $5,000 bonus to the girl who brings on board the most new recruits who do pass said probation. We need more bodies out there, enough so that we're not simply working to save up the principal.

Netflix has chosen this exact moment to bail on me. Three red dots repeatedly run across the centre of the pitch black screen from left to right, like ever-replenishing blood droplets falling into a cruel and unforgiving abyss. An abyss which holds back promises of more peaceful times in plain sight while dripping more red en route to a destination I'll never see.

The crimson drops hit my eyes hard with cold flashes of darkness. Raven, Buford, Nile. Each red circle fades but soon resurfaces, like an indelible sin which lives on in a deep crevice of the psyche long after the physical evidence of the act has faded put of sight. How many more dots will fall, and is there really a paradise beyond the bloodshed?

My phone buzzes. It's Redclay.

'Are you ready? We've got him.'

CHAPTER 40

A sparse warehouse. Eery silence and empty spaces breathing discomfort where one would normally find peace. Chipped white paint on the walls exposes blotches of rusted metal. All around me I see cracks and crevices. The windows high up adjoining the walls to the ceiling allow in some supplementary light.

Muldoon is tied to a table staring at the ceiling, Lalo, one of Diana's loyal rent-a-bangers, and I standing either side of him while Diana stands in front. All three of us wear ski masks, my glasses clinging to my ears on the inside. Each of us loiter and intimidate while firmly gripping a gun.

'Officer Muldoon, you're most troublesome for a lowly patrolman.' I affect a throaty, gravelly growl as I say this, almost channelling a bad Batman caricature. 'Why are you so interested in Jeremy Goldstein and his associates? We've been watching you. You've been hanging around the university hospital, keeping tabs on that hooker who was in the car crash with Brad Thunberg. Whose crew are you working for?'

'What? Crew?' Every syllable trembles with trepidation.

'Don't play the innocent with me. We saw you on the phone. Who were you talking to?'

'Roy. Roy Raganathan. Special Agent Raganthan. FBI.'

This is far worse than I could have imagined. The FBI have eyes on Goldstein, and we're a speck of dust on that picture which they'll happily swat en route to the real prize. This isn't our fight per se, but we could very well end up shedding blood.

'What does he know and what is he planning?'

'He's been trying to build a RICO case against Goldstein for years. No luck. He has the names of everybody connected to Top Drawer Entertainment, including the owners. It was through Emily that he connected the business to Goldstein. Half the girls there worked for Raven Garcia, including Emily. Raven was a courier for Goldstein and was trying to come up as a distributor.'

'Nice exposition.' Diana. Very droll.

'Why are you helping him?' I ask.

'We're friends. We go way back. High school.'

Touching.

'What's his next move?'

'As soon as Emily comes around, he's going to offer her a deal. He'll make the solicitation charge and her now violated probation go away if she agrees to wear a wire.'

'A wire?'

'Yeah. He wants it all. Top Drawer, Garcia, and Goldstein. Roy always gets his man.'

'Bullshit. You don't even have enough for the solicitation charge.'

'We found a stack of C-notes in Emily's bra, one of which Brad Thunberg was kind enough to autograph.'

Dumb fucking jock.

'That proves nothing.'

That proves almost everything.

'Trust me, we've got what we need for the charge to stick. Eyewitnesses, surveillance footage from the hotel, everything. Roy's got your boy Goldstein's balls under a hot tap and you know it.'

He's right. I've got a handful of nothing but I don't want to show him my cards.

'Emily won't talk.'

'Are you kidding? She's looking at real hard time. Deportation too as soon as she's done in the slammer. I guarantee it.'

Don't sell it.

'You think she's doing a stretch for you? No way. Never.'

He's got us on the ropes. The hand holding the towel is raised high but I'm not ready to throw it in just yet.

'Talk to Ray. Stall the investigation.'

'Roy.'

'Whatever.'

'The wheels are in motion. Roy's mind is made up and he's not going to change it. The ink is drying on the draft copy of Emily's deal as I speak. If I try to call Roy off he'll be nothing but suspicious and he'll ask even more questions.'

Torching the hornet's nest may just send the buzz of black and yellow flying in all directions with a heightened fervour. What if the hive stays unfettered while our machinations slowly unfold in the distance?

'He really trusts you.'

'Of course. We talk every single day.'

'You're a good cop. Honest. Incorruptible. Not good enough to make Detective.'

'What?'

Now we have his balls under a hot tap.

'Who have you been talking to?'

'You're a boy scout. A patsy. It got you nowhere. But what if we could change that?'

'Are you trying to bribe me?'

Silence. Let the possibilities stew in his mind.

'How would you like to be one of Diana Redclay's detectives in Vice?'

'Vice?'

'Redclay does what we tell her to do. We run things there. If you do for us, we will do for you. If you don't then we will make life very difficult for you.'

'What do you want?'

'Stop Raganathan from making a deal with Emily, one way or another.'

'I told you already, Roy is not for turning.'

'That's one way. Try another.'

'Another?'

'Yes.'

'I don't understand.'

Deep breath. Eyes closed. Stare into the darkness and pray that a slither of light stares back. If it doesn't then simply accept the eyes which do and follow the devil's gaze.

'If Raganathan won't change his mind then we will make him talking to Emily a physical impossibility.'

'A physical impossibility?'

'Yes. When I said we, I meant that you would be the one to do it.'

The devil's gaze burns hard, extending a flaming hand and waiting for the touch paper to return the gesture.

'Consider this the Detective's exam.'

'What do you want me to do?'

When the flame hits the touch paper it ignites the fire and unburdens itself of the responsibility for what's to come.

'There can be no deal with only one party around to make it.'

'Wait, are you seriously suggesting that I murder Emily?'

Staring back into the darkness. Once again no light looks back. Only a trail of blood can lead me out of the damask.

'You know what needs to happen, so go out there and make it happen.'

Muldoon shudders and shakes his head. The mere suggestion of what he thinks I want him to do has him clearly perturbed.

'Consider this your audition. If you pass this test then there's a regular role for you.'

Silence. He's still thinking about the last thing that I didn't say.

'Raganathan trusts you, so he'll believe anything that you tell him. From now on you tell him what we well you to. You do that and soon you'll be a detective with a sergeant's pay grade.'

He nods silently and diffidently. Part focus and part fear.

'But first you audition. You've got until Sunday. Just get it done.'

He lets out a nervous sigh.

'In case you're wondering, the hole in the desert with your name on it has already been dug in case you back out.'

CHAPTER 41

I stare at Muldoon's name and number on my phone screen. My mind weighs heavy with the words we exchanged a few nights ago. I've got half a mind to text him and call everything off. It would be the humane thing to do. The moral thing. The right thing. But we didn't end up here because we did what's right, and doing right now will only hasten our demise.

When the line in the sand has been drawn in blood, one can only survive on the other side by drawing more red. Lola knows nothing of this. She can never know, and neither can the girls. Not now. Not ever. As far as they'll be concerned Emily will die from a heart attack brought about by her various injuries from the crash. They will never know the truth.

But I will.

I'm doing this for each and every one of them. They have no idea of the line of fire that they're standing in, and because of me they'll never have to. Because of me they get to sleep on obliviously as the armed intruder quietly flees the scene, unnerved by a bump in the night. I'm the one who bumped so that we could all stay afloat.

One text is all it will take to spare a life, but by sparing those few flicks of my thumb I can save all of us and everything we've worked so hard to build up. Emily doesn't deserve this. She's a loyal professional who ended up here because she did her job. But what does deserving have to do with anything? Besides, I didn't put her up there in Thunberg's room. Lola and I gave that job to Gabriella. She decided to make it a triple threat match before taking her ball and going home. If anything the blood will be on her hands.

But she will never know.

The group chat is buzzing with activity. Our girls are taking the recruitment drive very seriously, each and every one of them pledging to donate their bonuses to Emily's family back in Romania. They're kind people with good hearts. If they knew what was coming, well, I can't even begin to imagine the blowback. It could just as easily be any one of them.

I will make things right. I'll put a million dollars into a bank account for Emily's family. The money won't bring back their cherished Emily, but unlike me throwing myself on my own sword it will help her family and serve the purpose of Emily's work here. She came here for the betterment of her family. I will finish her work, and that's a promise.

The recruitment drive is really gathering steam. The girls are really going for it and they will have at least two potential new recruits each before the weekend.

We're going to be very busy with interviews between now and the end of next week. Hopefully, I'll be able to help Lola with next week's interviews. We need new girls, ones who will not be hit hard by Emily's passing and can earn big money from next week.

Two girls each would give us thirty, enough for four new locations. Pretty soon the money hole left by the looming grief of our current crew will be but a distant memory. Plus, when the time is right, we will have to replace Emily. I know it sounds callous, but at the end of the day we are running a business. The name of the game is making money.

A dead in the water FBI investigation as a result of this decision, not to mention the deed itself, will give me something to talk about with Goldstein. The damage which could have been caused by a successful FBI probe would have cost Goldstein considerably more than the sum we owe him at present. That right there is reason enough for Jeremy to write off the debt. Once this Emily situation has been taken care of, I want a sit-down with Goldstein. Not Harley, not another of his minions. Goldstein himself.

I don't mind paying Goldstein a fair tribute. It's a cost of doing business in his town. But the current situation is not sustainable. In return for that tribute we would expect protection of our territory from Goldstein and his organization. Our business savvy and Goldstein's fearsome reputation are all the tools we need to take over this town. Vegas could be ours for the taking, but none of that will be possible unless we take care of this Emily situation.

The road to respite often goes through brutality. Just as the road to my current subversive state was paved by years to tedium, boredom and frustration.

The office Christmas party. Those annual tedium Olympics. Watching people all around you get mad drunk while filling the silences between myself and the few other people in the sober category with laborious small talk. Raj has had a few pints of lager and is now telling anyone regardless of whether they will listen or not how he was there the day that Manchester United beat Arsenal 6-2. Oh how I'd love to slap his face and knock his wig into his dessert.

I'm so bored right now. The rubber chicken dinner now consumed, I contemplate excusing myself to go to the gents and not returning. I'm OK with spending the rest of the night back in my hotel room reading Emily Bronte's poetry and watching TV. To think that I walked away from a decent *Columbo* marathon on ITV2 for this mediocre party.

This Christmas party would be different from all the others, or so we were told. Employees from all of the company's multiple divisions would be there. In previous years staff from the non-Relocation business lines, including Records Management, were not invited to the Christmas party. This despite the fact that we share office space. When the General Manager announced this revolutionary idea he acted as though he'd just spun gold.

My colleague to my left, Derek, is very drunk and very loud, bleating on about how 'Yid Army' is not an offensive chant. He's been pounding them down like they're going out of fashion since we accidentally met up in the bar with Les and Chiwetel beforehand and ended up watching the Spurs match before dinner. He grows more annoying with each passing drink.

'Yid Army!'

Yes, that actually just happened.

Derek has this awful party trick, and an accurate description of him when he does it would be a portmanteau of the words party and trick. He loves to pull out the Spurs jersey tucked into his suit trousers, throw it on, stand up with his arms in the air and shout 'Yid Army!' whenever we're at a function.

I grab a bottle of red wine from the middle of the table and pour myself a hearty glass. After taking a deep breath I gulp down a sharp mouthful of rouge, sending a strange shudder through my head and torso. What's the worst that could happen.

Pacing the strip from Aria to Treasure Island, nervous, restless, feeling the full dragging weight of each early morning minute. I've made this return journey once on foot already after stopping off at Aria for a couple of Courvoisiers. The thought-dulling effect of the raw liquid fire would normally be anathema to me, but right now it comes as a sweet welcome release.

Remnants of more frivolous thoughts and memories float back to the surface of my mind as a giddy weightless feeling hits me between the ears. Each happy thought eventually fades to a cruel death after flying too close to the sun of a harsh reality. A sun imbued by the darkness of tough decisions immediately before us.

A Treasure Island vodka Martini from a clear plastic cup put some bright clouds between that dark sun and the present moment, clouds which clear just as quickly as they emanated. Soon enough my mind veers back towards the proliferation of calls and messages from Lola which I have so far ignored.

Diana has also been blowing up my phone like crazy. She has a very nervous Muldoon to contend with and needs to placate him. That means I need to placate her. I'm not a fucking guidance counsellor. Muldoon was called upon to do a job and he was well incentivized to do it. I even agreed to pay him $50,000 cash up front with the promise of a further $10,000 upon completion. I will happily deliver the ten grand to him at his home later on today, provide that he keeps it together, does what he's told and doesn't fuck up between now and then. He knows what needs to happen now. I'm not going to tell him again.

The synthetic morning air breathes a deceptively welcoming scent of jasmine fused with vanilla. I pass two hot-panted young women on the bridge as *Just an Illusion* by Imagination begins to play. A year ago, I would have struggled to conjure an illusion that looked anything like this, but today for better or worse it is reality.

During these creaking hours the Strip is uncharacteristically and unnervingly quiet. The veneer of vivacious pomp and pizzazz adopts an ominous grey, as though I'm now looking at the funhouse with blood in my eyes. The blood of an innocent woman. Those old familiar sights are all the same, except the neon lights now drip with death, destruction and creeping despair.

I keep going back and forth in my mind regarding the pros and cons of killing Emily. Sure, she's a sister, daughter, aunt and friend. She doesn't deserve this. I didn't put her in that car with Thunberg and I most certainly didn't crash it. Every time I draw up that ledger the balancing entry is one of self-preservation.

I'll talk to Lola when I get home. Tell her that I needed to clear my concussed head. She doesn't need to know that I've been clearing it with alcohol. I'll need a strong black coffee before going back. I should probably avoid the Treasure Island Starbucks and Lola's friend Amy. But first I could do with a Coors. Or two.

All the alcohol and lists and soul-searching in the world won't make a jot of difference. It may briefly change the way I feel about the Emily decision, sure, but it won't change the necessity for and ramifications of it.

Especially now that Emily has been dead for over an hour and a half.

END OF VOLUME I

Printed in Great Britain
by Amazon

31405335R00205